SHADOW OF THE NOOSE

Toby Small is determined to prove his brother innocent of the murder of a US marshal by tracking down the real killer. But his quest proves dangerous when the foreman of the Crooked L ranch goes for his gun ... With more problems ahead, Small is helped by the feisty Ella and adventurer Ray. But by showdown time even Ray will have had his fill of danger and violence. Can Toby save his brother and bring justice to Snake City against all the odds?

SYDNEY J. BOUNDS

SHADOW OF THE NOOSE

Complete and Unabridged

LINFORD
Leicester

First published in Great Britain in 2001

First Linford Edition
published 2008

British Library CIP Data

Bounds, Sydney J.
    Shadow of the noose.—Large print ed.—
Linford western library
    1. Western stories
    2. Large type books
    I. Title
    823.9'14 [F]

    ISBN 978–1–84782–050–1

Published by
F. A. Thorpe (Publishing)
Anstey, Leicestershire

Set by Words & Graphics Ltd.
Anstey, Leicestershire
Printed and bound in Great Britain by
T. J. International Ltd., Padstow, Cornwall

This book is printed on acid-free paper

1

Scream for Help

Toby rarely felt embarrassed. He prided himself he could eel out of any situation with a smile and a line of patter. But a crying woman floored him.

It didn't help that she was expecting, and showed it. Neither did it help that she really had something to cry about.

'You've got to help, Toby!'

She sounded desperate and he reached out and rested his hand on hers. 'Of course I will, Polly. You know that. It's why you sent for me.'

The kitchen was so tiny that, even with the back door open, he felt trapped. She was rolling pastry for a pudding and had a smudge of flour on her nose and her hair was wild as uncoiled wire.

He pushed away his empty plate and

picked up the mug as she refilled it with coffee.

'I can let you have twenty bucks to tide you over.'

'It's not just the money, Toby. George didn't do it no matter what anybody says.'

'Of course he didn't.'

It was difficult not to laugh. The idea of his holier-than-thou brother shooting anyone was enough to make a clown smile.

'You must get him out!'

His brother's wife was plump and cuddly, but not very bright. Well, she'd married George, hadn't she? And George was in jail.

'I'll have a word with the sheriff.'

'But he's the one who arrested him. Mr Nash believes he's guilty.'

He'd always considered his sister-in-law an attractive woman, but her present tear-streaked face spoilt the memory.

'Polly, I've only just got into town. I don't know any details yet. Let me see what I can find out, then we'll decide how best to help George.'

A sudden breeze brought the scent of flowers from the garden; it clashed with the pungent smell of a polish. Toby had no doubt it was George who did the polishing.

He gulped his coffee and pushed back his chair. He wasn't doing any good here.

'I'll see you later. Trust me.'

As Polly began crying again, he left by the back door. He hoped she washed her face before she went to see her husband, and felt glad he'd booked a room at the hotel.

He walked down an alley to Main Street and paused on the boardwalk to take a long breath. Polly in trouble was wearing. How on earth, he wondered, had the idiot managed to get himself accused of murder?

Toby took his time walking along the main throughway of Snake City. The town was the biggest in the area simply because it was on the railroad and easily reached; it had grown since his last visit. He passed the church and a bank, a school and the courthouse; the sheriff lived next door to the jail.

'Toby Small to see his brother.'

The sheriff nodded. 'Why not? Sure sorry for the man's wife.'

He led Toby back from his office and opened a cell door. 'I'm locking you in — let me know when you're done talking.'

The door slammed, a key turned.

'Hello, George.'

His brother glared at him. 'I suppose you think this is funny? You're the crook in the family — you're the one who should be here in my place!'

Toby grinned, and perched on the edge of the bunk. George was older, with thinning hair and round shoulders. He had stubble on his chin.

'Better call a truce and give me your side of things if we're going to get yuh out.'

Idly, he ran a hand over the stone slab of the wall. There were iron bars across a glassless window, and a bucket in the corner.

George paced the flagstone floor. 'I've told the sheriff this situation is absurd. I heard shots and ran to see if I could help . . . '

'Where was this? When?'

'Right on Main Street, in the evening. I'd just come from a church meeting, and I saw a body lying in the road. The man was plainly dead when I reached him, and I saw a revolver on the ground beside him. I picked it up — and the sheriff appeared and arrested me.'

'Sounds reasonable,' Toby said.

'It's not at all reasonable!' George shouted. 'I was trying to help. After all, I'm a well-known member of the church.'

Toby grinned. 'For once, a do-gooder gets it in the neck! Sounds about right, George — you always did poke your nose in where it wasn't wanted.'

'Very funny!'

George continued packing the stone flags. Four paces, about turn, four paces back. Toby reflected: at least it should get some of the weight off him.

'Did you notice anybody else about before the sheriff arrived?'

George frowned. 'There was some-one — hardly more than a shadow disappearing into an alleyway. No one I could recognize.'

'Pity.'

'I can't seem to convince the sheriff of the seriousness of his error.'

'I'd say he doesn't believe it is an error.'

George paused and stared at him. 'Toby, you can't mean . . . ?'

Toby shook his head. 'Of course not, George. I believe you're too innocent for your own good and I'll do whatever I can to set you straight.'

'Just get me out. I don't like it here!'

'I'll try.'

Toby knocked on the cell door. Sheriff Nash opened it and he walked free.

'Still saying he didn't do it?'

Nash was an old-timer with a moustache the colour of walnut; he covered the entire county, with a couple of deputies.

'Yes, and I believe him. I've known George most of his life, and he'd no more shoot a man than burn down his church. He's real pain at times.'

Toby leaned casually against a wall, his gaze roaming around the office, studying the type of lock, the thickness of the door, the keys hanging from a wall rack.

It was the sort of assessment that came naturally to him.

'Don't even think it,' Nash warned, lifting a shotgun from behind his desk. 'You get him on the run and he'll be hunted down and killed.'

Toby nodded agreement. 'Sometimes jail is the safest place.'

Nash replaced the shotgun, and picked up a knife to cut a slice from a plug of tobacco; he put it in his mouth and chewed.

'I found him holding the gun, standing over the body. A Colt revolver, recently fired. Man shot twice in the back — sure obvious who done it.'

'I'm not blaming you, Sheriff. Likely I'd take the same view in your boots — but I ain't, and I know George. He never could kill a spider, or a mouse.'

Toby stayed calm and relaxed. Nash was honest, but mule-headed. When he took a notion, he stuck to it; arguing would only make him surer than ever that he was right.

'Nobody else about at the time, I suppose?'

'If there had been before, once the shooting started they'd be long gone.' Nash paused. 'No fear of a lynching, so let him stay where he is and take his chance at the trial.'

He shifted his tobacco from one side of his mouth to the other.

''Course we didn't know then who the dead man was. Just a stranger in town. Found out later he was a United States marshal by the name of Beaumont. Shooting a lawman is likely to be taken real serious by the judge.'

'Likely enough,' Toby agreed, and

walked outside into the sunlight.

He continued along the boardwalk, past the pool hall and a meat market, till he reached a sign: JACKSON'S GENERAL STORE. That, too, had grown since he was last here. It was where George worked, or had.

As he entered the dim coolness, he smelled soap and leather, tobacco and coffee, and saw that Jackson had already taken on another man to replace his brother.

He helped himself to a cracker from the barrel and munched on it while he waited for the storeowner to finish serving a customer.

Jackson turned a wary gaze towards him. 'You're Toby Small.'

'That's right. I'm trying to find out what happened with George. Did you see anything?'

Jackson shook his head. 'Not a thing. I heard shots and kept my head down.'

A pity George didn't, Toby thought. 'Whereabouts was this?'

'Down the street a way — near

enough opposite the Longhorn.'

Jackson got behind his counter, as if for protection; he moved carefully because he was getting middle-aged spread and crates of goods left little room.

'Can you arrange credit for Polly?' Toby asked.

'I can if you're paying. I run a business, not a charity for widows and orphans.'

Toby handed the store-owner twenty dollars in coin. 'That should cover it for a while. You'll be taking George back when he gets out, I suppose?'

Jackson looked at him as if he were mad. 'You haven't heard?'

Toby gazed steadily at him, and Jackson said, 'The circuit judge this time round is Benson.'

As Toby left the store, his heart sank. Benson was well known as 'a hanging judge.'

2

The Holy Joe

George Small continued to pace the stone flags of his cell after Toby left. The heavy door slammed and a key turned in the lock with a finality that sent a shiver along his spine. Sunlight cast bars of shadow across his face.

Temptation eased through a chink in his armour and he thought: wouldn't it be nice to exchange the keys to the Kingdom of Heaven for a key to *this* door?

It was infuriating. His brother, a confidence trickster who should have been caught and put in prison long ago, could walk out a free man. An innocent man, who'd never owned a gun in his life, was accused of murder. How could this happen?

In his pacing, he accidentally kicked

the half-full bucket in the corner, making him conscious of the smell he now almost took for granted. He shuddered. George was fastidious about cleanliness — even Polly joked about the amount of polish he got through.

He'd always resented Toby's easy acceptance of making a living without working, his success at taking money off honest folk with a few glib lies. While he worked hard in Jackson's store, giving an honest day's work for a day's pay. And he supported the church and paid his dues. It was enough to shake a man's faith. That was when he realized he was being tested, and he prayed for strength to surmount his ordeal.

Luckily Polly still believed in him and brought his dinner on a regular basis. But to be confined, pacing like an animal in a cage, disturbed him. Not to be allowed a razor to shave; he'd never before had bristles on his jaw. Nash even went so far as to deny him his walk to church service on Sunday morning!

It was beyond belief that he couldn't get the sheriff to see he was innocent. The man was a fool but, unfortunately, a fool with authority.

George found he was getting short of breath. Polly had always served large portions. He stopped pacing and lay on the bunk, uncomfortably aware that the blanket was none too clean. He stared up at the bars across the window, remembering that evening when he'd lost his freedom . . .

★　★　★

It had been a pleasantly warm evening, the shadows beginning to lengthen when he left the church after a committee meeting. He'd felt a glow of satisfaction. Sometimes, although meaning well, a few members of the church needed firm guidance. He was aware that he'd spoken well, and the decision to obtain a bell had gone his way.

In future, they would be able to ring

the faithful to church on a Sunday morning.

It was odd, he reflected, how other members of the committee always had some excuse to rush away, leaving him to walk alone. But it was late and he had no reason to hurry. He strolled along the boardwalk, wondering what Polly had for supper. George liked his food.

Only a few saloons had so far lit their lamps. It was that twilight hour between stores and workshops closing and the business of the night commencing. The air was balmy and, in the quiet, he heard the tinkling of a piano.

George frowned. Once again saloon-keepers would be about the business of the devil; liquor and cards and women who were no better than they ought to be. The church in Snake City hadn't enough supporters yet to insist the sheriff close these places, but the time would come. He had no doubt of that. As more settlers arrived, store-people and farmers and honest tradesmen, the

14

church would grow stronger and . . .

Shots echoed through the silence; two, close together. George paused, heart in his mouth. It was not often the town had a shooting, he'd believed those days were in the past.

He peered into the gathering dusk; it was difficult to make things out clearly, but the street appeared almost deserted.

He glimpsed the back of a man moving quickly into the dark mouth of an alley, and a form sprawled unmoving in the dust in the middle of Main Street.

He hurried forward, leaving the boardwalk. Possibly someone needed help — and, as a good citizen, it was his duty to investigate this breach of the peace and inform the sheriff.

He reached the body, lying in a spreading pool of blood, face down. By the light from a nearby saloon, the man looked beyond help.

Curious, George picked up the gun lying beside the body and inspected it.

'All right,' a voice said from behind

him. 'Give me that and stick your hands in the air.'

George turned, startled. Sheriff Nash had a revolver in his hand, pointed at him. Automatically, George handed over the weapon as a deputy ran up.

'Watch this one,' Nash said, and knelt to study the body in the dust.

The deputy had his own gun out, scowling. 'Grab the moon, feller!'

The corpse was that of a big man, a Colt still holstered at his waist and a Stetson half off his head.

'Dead enough for any undertaker. And shot in the back — twice, to make sure.'

Nash straightened up, eyeing George with contempt. 'I hate a backshooter. Start walking to the jailhouse. You're under arrest.'

George gaped. 'Me? Surely you don't think I shot this man?'

'It's obvious, I'd say. Only you here, and holding the gun.' Nash sniffed at the muzzle. 'Yep, this one.'

George glanced down at the body.

'But I've never seen him before.'

'So you say. For that matter, neither have I. We'll find out who he is — was — later.' Nash prodded him into motion. 'Or maybe you're saying someone else just happened to drop this gun here?'

'I suppose . . . '

The deputy gave him a shove in the middle of his back. 'Quit supposing and move!'

'This is stupid! I'm George Small — of course, I didn't shoot him — I give you my word.'

'Tell it to the judge,' Nash growled. 'My job's only to catch 'em. You got anything to say, save it for the trial.' He nodded to his deputy. 'No need to bother the doc. Just get the undertaker to remove the body.'

'Right.'

At the jail, the sheriff opened a stationery ledger he used to book in prisoners, and took up a pen.

'Name and address?'

'Really, Sheriff, you know who I am

and where I live. Look, Polly is expecting me back for supper about now.'

'Should have thought of your wife before. Empty your pockets.' Nash made an inventory of his possessions. 'In here.'

He unlocked a cell door and, when George appeared reluctant to enter, gave him a shove.

'This is your home till the circuit judge gets to us.'

As he slammed the door, he added, 'It's Benson this time round.'

George stood motionless in the cell, bemused and bewildered. He had yet to take in his situation fully. There was a bunk, with a single blanket and bolster, and a bucket in one corner. His nose wrinkled.

He sat down, his legs suddenly weak; he was beginning to feel scared. He'd heard of Judge Benson; in fact, approved of his attitude — for criminals.

Despite his innocence, when he looked at the bars across the window, he shivered.

3

Voices in the Dark

Toby waited until dusk and the oil lamps were lit in the Longhorn, the nearest saloon to where the marshal had been gunned down. He paused briefly to study the street and found it difficult to make out any detail.

Heads turned as he pushed through the batwings. Eyes stared, some with animosity. Talk died away. They knew who he was and, perhaps, one of them knew rather more than that.

Toby was tall with the build of an athlete and didn't carry a gun openly. His suit was good-quality broadcloth, a bit worn and still dusty from the trail; he always bought the best quality when he could — it lasted longer.

He moved steadily to the bar and said, 'A small beer, please.'

The barman served him in silence and Toby paid. No one spoke to him as he leaned back against the counter and sipped his drink, watching closely over the rim of his glass.

He recognized only one face: Jackson's. One or two he remembered vaguely from past visits, but most were new and unknown.

He sighed. 'All right, you know who I am and why I'm here. Did anybody see anything?'

Nobody answered till a burly man left the billiard table and pushed past the card players towards him. He carried a cue, smacking the thick end into the palm of his hand.

'We know who yuh are — and we ain't going to let yuh unload your bible-punching brother's killing on to us. Sheriff caught him red-handed and that's it. We heard shots — it was over before anyone looked out of the window and saw Nash had his man.'

A pity George couldn't mind his own business as well, Toby thought.

The burly man's lip curled. 'A backshooter. Just try accusing anyone here and you'll buy trouble.'

A few other drinkers made approving noises; one or two looked threatening.

'I'm not accusing anyone,' Toby said mildly. 'Just trying to find out what happened.'

'Your goody-goody brother shot a US marshal is what happened.' The man with the cue crowded him against the counter. 'If he don't swing, another marshal will get him.'

Silence descended again. Someone spat close to Toby's boots.

'You might as well leave,' growled a voice from the back of the room.

Toby shrugged and finished his beer. 'Guess you're right. Seems nobody here knows a thing.'

As he moved towards the door a voice jeered and he ignored it. He felt he was wasting his time, and made up his mind to quit Snake City in the morning. He'd try the homesteads on the road in and out of town. But first he had to see Polly.

★ ★ ★

Not many lamps were still burning even in the saloons. The heat of day had dispersed and the night noises with it. Now it was cooler, sleep was possible. A couple of drunks weaved unsteadily along Main Street, propping each other up.

Shadows, black as soot, lined an alleyway. Two figures froze until the drunks passed. Voices whispered.

'Well?'

'Small's brother is snooping. He was in the Longhorn, asking questions.'

'So?' This voice held more than a hint of impatience.

'Seems to me he's not the kind to quit asking questions till he gets some answers.'

'Too bad for him.' This time there was the hint of a sneer. 'If he makes a nuisance of himself, I'll have someone take care of him.'

'Do you want me to — ?'

'No.' The voice was sharp. 'I don't

want any link between that damned marshal and us. Wait. This brother may give up — especially if the judge arrives sooner rather than later.'

'Maybe.' The other voice held an element of doubt.

'If he doesn't, arrange it out of town. And find someone else to attend to it.'

A shadowy figure moved away. Then the other merged with the night. Footfalls faded. The dark alley became as silent as Boot Hill.

★ ★ ★

Polly was beginning to feel she could cope again, after Toby promised to help. George was all right but, at times, a little distant from reality; his brother was more down to earth and familiar with the ways of the world.

She felt that, if anyone could help, then he could — even though George was always running him down. After all, blood was thicker than water.

Her husband was in a complaining

mood when she collected an empty dish, but he hadn't lost his appetite despite the threat hanging over him.

'Where's Toby? What's he doing? Is he doing anything to get me out of here?'

'He saw me late last night. He hasn't found anybody who saw what really happened. Now he's going round the outlying farms.'

George snorted. 'He's wasting time!'

Polly refrained from pointing out that not one of his church friends had offered any help at all. They were keeping well clear of this mess.

As she withdrew, the deputy locked the cell door after her. She went outside and found the sheriff taking his ease in the sun; his chair was tilted back and he chewed on a wad of tobacco.

Polly paused. 'Why can't you see there's no reason for my husband to shoot a federal marshal?'

'You don't know everything he got up to before yuh married him, Mrs Small.'

She heard the whistle of a train

arriving, and turned towards the depot to see a cloud of steam and smoke, and small children running excitedly to admire the huge locomotive.

Nash took out his watch. 'On time, sure enough.'

A buckboard waited near the depot as the train shuddered to a halt with a screeching of brakes. The driver of the wagon, dressed as a cowboy, with a gunbelt and flat-crowned hat pulled low, jumped down to meet passengers coming off the train.

Nash squinted into the glare. 'That's Carver, foreman at the Crooked L. Interesting the way that ranch manages to keep going.' He spat a stream of brown tobacco juice. 'Relies on dudes paying board for a vacation out West. Guess he's meeting another of them, and they'll stay overnight at the hotel and leave town in the morning.'

Polly said quickly, 'Did Carver stay overnight the evening the marshal was shot?'

Nash snorted. 'Don't give up, do yuh? Frankly, I don't know — I've no reason to keep track of folk meeting trains. But I can tell yuh Carver fancies himself as a gunfighter and wouldn't take kindly to being called a back-shooter. Or be careless enough to drop his gun afterwards.'

'Could it be one of the Easterners?'

The sheriff laughed outright. 'Give it up, Mrs Small. The killer's in jail and that's where he'll stay till the trial.' He walked away.

Polly stayed a bit longer, watching the new arrivals. It seemed she had little to do nowadays; her life was in limbo.

She saw Carver, a handsome man, move towards a smartly dressed passenger and speak to him; the foreman collected a trunk and loaded it on to the buckboard. They drove towards the hotel.

Carver halted the wagon on Main Street, outside the bank, one of the few stone buildings in Snake City; his hat-brim was pulled well down to shield his eyes.

She saw the banker, Chancellor, step outside; a man as solid as his bank. Carver introduced the visitor. There were smiles and handshakes and a brief dialogue before the wagon moved on.

Polly wondered what it would be like to have the kind of money needed for a vacation half-way across the continent, sighed, and turned for home.

She had at least to go through the motions of living. But the scene stayed with her and nagged away: Carver, the Easterner, and Chancellor.

4

No Trouble in Tumbleweed

Toby was away at first light, knowing that farmers would be working in their fields. At the livery stable he hitched his two mules to the wagon and drove out of town. The wagon, with its canvas hood, was more than a means of transport; it was his home for most of the year and held everything he owned and needed for survival.

Millie and Monty were more than just draught animals; they were his friends and he talked to them when he crossed the empty plains between towns. The mules moved at a stately gait but, when necessary, could show their heels to would-be pursuers.

Toby accepted that he wasn't likely to get far with his enquiries in Snake City. Most people took the sheriff's arrest at face value. But, he reflected, the killer had to come from somewhere and go somewhere afterwards — and small farms started just beyond the town limits.

He realized George would be out of luck if the killer had travelled by railroad. The unknown one could be anywhere by now.

Someone must know something, and he wanted to find whoever had the information he wanted. Who did it? And why? And what was a United States marshal doing in Snake City?

This fact argued against a casual shooting and for a known outlaw. A cold-blooded assassination. Revenge? To stop an investigation?

Toby paused at each house he came to and delivered his rapid-fire sales pitch:

'And how's your back today, ma'am? I have here my own patented cure-all — guaranteed to relieve any ache or pain. A sure-fire thing and a bargain at a dollar a bottle. Trust me, ma'am. To you, fifty cents.'

And into his patter, he dropped the vital question: 'Have you seen any strangers riding into or out of town recently. Or heard about any from your neighbours?'

He repeated this with variations: 'How's your leg, sir? My pain-elixir attacks lumbago and arthritis to provide instant relief' without getting any useful information. No strangers in the night. No visitors.

Except the Easterners, the dudes travelling out to the Crooked L ranch.

He considered this intelligence thoughtfully. Any visitor from the East meant money, and money could buy a smart lawyer. If he was up against that, his job would be doubly difficult.

He was past the last straggling homestead when a voice hailed him.

'Hi, mister. Will yuh give me a lift along the way?'

Toby glanced down to see a boy of, he guessed, about fourteen standing beside the track. He wore cast-offs a size too big; a farmer's boy by the look of him, but cleaner than some. He had a cheerful grin and freckles and carried a knife in a sheath clipped to his belt.

'Sure, jump on. How far yuh going?'

'Going to see the elephant,' the boy said.

Toby smiled. 'What's your name, son?'

'Ray.'

'Waal, Ray, you call me Toby. Parents know you're leaving?'

The grin faded. 'They're dead. I live with my sister.'

'Hope you're looking after her.'

'She thinks she's looking after me! Now she's got a sweetheart . . . where yuh going, Toby?'

'Here and there. No fixed destination, no fixed abode. Where the wind blows me. I sell cure-alls, play cards for money, a bit of this and a bit of that.'

Ray grinned as if he approved. 'Bet you've had lots of adventures! Think Indians will attack us?'

'Sure hope not. Be a mite difficult to

form a circle with only one wagon.'

They drove on in silence, then Ray said, 'You've got good mules. I know about mules.'

'They have names — Millie and Monty. D'you know anything about a US marshal getting himself shot in town?'

'Not heard that,' Ray admitted.

Toby thought a boy's natural curiosity might ferret something out. 'Waal, keep your eyes open. And if you hear anything, let me know.'

'You a lawman, or something?'

'Or something,' Toby said. 'D'you know this ranch where the Eastern dudes stay?'

'Know of it — out Tumbleweed way.'

The land went on, seemingly endless, mostly flat with minor undulations, short brown grass, the bend of a river in the distance, uninhabited huts where homesteaders had given up. Toby drove on till he reached the small town called Tumbleweed.

He noted saloons and stores, a new

lick of paint giving them an air of prosperity; the town marshal's office, and one building with a door set between two glass windows. Signs claimed one half to be a newspaper office and the other half a photographer's studio.

He drew up at the livery stable adjoining a hotel, unhitched Millie and Monty and gave instructions about their feeding.

The stableman stared at him, and sniffed.

'Mules?'

'You got something against mules, feller? These are friends of mine.'

'No sir, mules are fine by me.'

Toby collected a carpet-bag with his personal gear and walked towards the hotel. 'D'you have any plans, Ray? Any money?'

'Not much money.'

Toby nodded. 'All right, you're working for me. Keep your eyes and ears open.'

He went into the hotel and booked a

room with two beds, climbed the stairs and dumped his gear. The room smelled of stale sweat and he opened the window.

With Ray tagging along, he went downstairs and crossed the dirt street to a dining-room. They were the only customers at this time of day and got immediate service. The table and the food was plain, but there was enough to satisfy the appetite of a growing boy.

Toby was lingering over a second mug of coffee when a gaunt man walked in. He came directly to their table; there was a badge pinned prominently to his coat and he carried a shotgun.

'My name's Lee. I've been appointed town marshal, and I check out all new arrivals. I'm here to let yuh know we don't like troublemakers here.'

He looked at Ray with suspicion. 'A runaway?'

Toby said smoothly, 'No trouble, Marshal. I'm just a travelling salesman, earning my bread. Here today and gone tomorrow. This lad is my apprentice, learning the trade. I'd appreciate it if you'll sit awhile and join us in a coffee and tell us about your fine town.'

Lee scowled. 'You've been warned. Keep inside the law, or move.' He left abruptly.

Toby paid the bill and went to the door and watched the marshal walk towards his office. He was used to the rough edge of the law, but this warning-off came too suddenly. Almost as if he were expected.

He said, absently, 'If you're tired, Ray, you can go up to our room and get some sleep.'

'I'm not tired, Toby. Couldn't sleep this early anyway. I'm too excited, and I ain't got to get up at first light like on the farm.'

Toby nodded. 'All right, sniff around town for a bit, but try to stay out of trouble. We don't want to upset Mr Lee.'

He watched the boy dash across the street and vanish into the stable, then he strolled along the boardwalk till he came to the biggest saloon in town. An ornate sign proclaimed it to be the Silver Spur.

It looked as though the old part had been smaller; now it seemed to have been repaired and painted and added to recently.

He pushed through the batwings and saw that the interior had also been spruced up. A large mirror in a fancy gilt frame reflected the painting of a naked woman on the opposite wall. Brass rails and spittoons shone.

A chandelier, the faceted glass refracting lights and colours from imported wine bottles, hung from a ceiling beam. Obviously the owner thought the trade from his Eastern visitors worth a bit of effort and expense.

There was no crowd yet, no dudes on view; just a few cowhands drinking at a table as they played cards, a sprinkling of townsmen.

Toby bought a beer and stood at the

counter, watching the card players, then he turned to the saloon-keeper and addressed him in a voice loud enough to be heard by everyone in the saloon.

'I've just driven in from Snake City. Did you hear that a federal marshal got himself shot dead? Right on Main Street.'

The saloon-keeper, a slight, balding man, looked sharply at him. 'No, sir, I hadn't heard that.'

The card players paused in their game to look towards him. They had the appearance of roughnecks rather than working cowboys, and they glanced at the man who was obviously their boss.

He wore a revolver at his waist and a flat-crowned hat pulled low; a handsome man except for his cold unwinking gaze. Toby was reminded of the hypnotic stare of a rattlesnake.

Their boss looked at Toby and gave a nod; one of the men pushed back his chair and stood up. He was short and wide with bulging muscles and short black hair. As the cowhand walked towards him Toby was reminded of a picture of a gorilla he'd once seen.

'What yuh trying to start, stranger? You want trouble? Maybe you'd best leave town sudden like?'

Someone laughed. 'Don't spill blood in here, Blackie. Take him outside in the alley.'

Another onlooker called to the saloon-keeper, 'Stay out of this, Paddy.'

Toby set down his glass on the counter and stepped right up close to Blackie as he waddled towards him. It seemed to the audience that he was stepping inside Blackie's great corded arms and would be crushed like an empty can. They watched expectantly.

A Derringer appeared in Toby's hand as if by magic, the twin muzzles almost touching Blackie's forehead.

'This little gun holds two forty-one-calibre slugs and is on a hair-trigger,' he said in a confidential tone. 'Fired this close, a bullet will give you an extra eye socket.'

The onlookers gasped, then shook

their heads in disbelief. No one had seen the stranger draw his gun.

'But not,' Toby said with regret, 'one that you could see out of.'

Blackie took a step backwards, almost crossing his eyes as he tried to focus his gaze on the twin muzzles. His face lost colour and his jaw seemed slack.

'Or do you prefer a cigar?' The Derringer vanished, as mysteriously as it had arrived, to be replaced by a fat cigar with a gold band around it. 'A quality item,' Toby assured him, smiling pleasantly. 'No five-cent smokes for my customers.'

Blackie took the cigar as if in a daze. 'How d'yuh do that?'

Toby struck a match and held it out. 'A little sleight of hand. All it takes is practice.'

Blackie stood in the centre of the Silver Spur, smoking the cigar. His mind was blank. He grasped the fact he had been outmanoeuvred, but had not the least idea what to do about it.

The batwings moved and two men strolled in. Their Western clothes were brand new with some fancy ornamentation.

The boss with staring eyes hissed, 'Come here, Blackie, and sit down.' He stood up, smiling, to give the dudes a friendly welcome.

Toby returned to the counter and finished his beer. 'The one giving orders, Paddy. Who's he?'

'That's Carver, foreman at the Crooked L. And I advise you don't try that stunt on him — he's got a reputation as a gunfighter.'

Toby nodded thoughtfully and asked for another beer. He figured he was safe enough while the dudes were in town.

The saloon-keeper served him and said, 'My name's O'Rourke, and I own this place, so here's another piece of advice — I don't appreciate strangers calling me 'Paddy'.'

5

Arrowhead

Excited, Ray ran into the stable to visit Toby's mules.

The stableman scowled at him. 'What yuh want here, kid?'

'Just checking on Millie and Monty,' he said, fondling their ears.

The stableman snorted. 'Giving mules names!'

Ray ignored him and looked around. 'You've sure got a lot of horses.'

'Some townsfolk keep their horses here — and I've got some I rent out to visitors.'

Ray checked Toby's wagon to make sure nothing had been tampered with, then ambled along Main Street. It was his first time in Tumbleweed and so an adventure, even if the place was much like his home town.

41

Shadows were gathering where stores closed their doors, leaving patches of darkness between the soft glow of oil-lamps from uncurtained windows. There were few people on the streets and no one bothered him until he reached a corner where some kids were tossing a coin and calling 'heads' or 'tails'.

One of them frowned at him. 'Who're you? You don't live here — what yuh doing in our town?'

'Just visiting,' Ray said loftily. 'I'm 'prenticed to a travelling salesman. You hear about the dead marshal of Snake City?'

'Tell us another! If that were true, it'd be in the paper.'

'You've got a paper?'

''Course we have!'

Ray recalled the double-fronted shop they'd passed on the way into town, and nodded. 'Guess I'd better see your printer if he's missing all the news.'

He headed for the newspaper office at a trot before the boys of Tumbleweed retaliated. He could hear the clanking of a hand-press at work as he approached. He pushed open the door.

Two oil-lamps burned this side of the shop; the photographic half was in darkness. There was a strong smell of ink.

'I've told you kids before, I don't want yuh in here when I'm working,' said an exasperated voice.

Ray paused on the threshold. A woman's voice!

'Thought yuh might want the latest from Snake City,' he said casually.

The printer straightened, turning from the press, and he saw she was young enough to remind him of his big sister, though with short blonde hair.

There was a smudge of ink on her forehead where she had pushed back her hair.

'Who are you, and what do you know? Quick now, I'm running off tomorrow's edition. I can insert a paragraph if you've got facts.'

'All I know is a US marshal was shot.

43

You want details, you'd better see Toby.'

'Who's Toby?'

'I'm riding along with him.'

'Name?'

'Ray.'

'Hello, Ray.' She smiled warmly. 'I'm Ella, and I'll run a paragraph now and give anything extra next time. I don't want to hold up this issue.'

He watched her set type with quick, darting fingers, and glanced at the title on the front page: the *Tumbleweed Trumpet*.

'How d'yuh get a job like this?' he asked, fascinated.

'I own the press, Ray. I'm reporter, editor and proof-reader all in one . . . does your family know where you are? Shouldn't you be in bed?'

Evasively, he said, 'I'm scouting for Toby. Guess I'd better go find him.'

'Well, I give a few cents for a story, Ray, if it's true. And tomorrow, I want words with your Mr Toby — be sure to tell him that.'

Polly was feeling low. She'd been sick that morning, and she worried about George, still in jail. She wondered where Toby was.

It seemed everyday things like cooking took much more effort, and George showed less and less appreciation. Of course, he had his own worries. What she really needed was a good heart-to-heart with another woman, but her friends didn't visit these days.

It was as she carried a covered dish along the boardwalk to the Snake City jailhouse, a regular chore now, that she met Dinah. An old friend from the church, Dinah had eaten more than one meal at their home.

Dinah had a basket of shopping on her arm as she came out of a store and they almost collided.

'Why, hello Dinah,' Polly said, brightening.

Dinah was a small, frail-seeming woman of uncertain age; birdlike, she darted glances all around, too embarrassed to look directly at her.

'Mrs Small, really . . . in Main Street too . . . perhaps it would be best if . . . everyone knows your husband is . . .'

Polly's back stiffened; her head snapped up. 'I thought you were our friend. I thought friends helped each other in times of trouble.'

Dinah pursed her lips. 'Your husband's brother should be here if you need help. You're his responsibility now.'

'Toby's busy looking for the real killer.'

Dinah sniffed and turned away, paused. 'I suppose you do know what they're saying? That the marshal and you . . .' She gave a delicate little laugh. 'I'm not saying I believe it, of course . . . and that's why your husband shot him . . .'

Polly could hardly take it in. She was no longer down, but almost spitting like a cat. She felt like hitting the woman.

'Who's saying that?' she demanded fiercely, ignoring the stares of passersby.

But Dinah, embarrassed, scurried away and Polly had to get to the jail. If George moaned about her food or his brother, she thought, she was in the mood to blister his ears.

★   ★   ★

Toby was wary when he left the Silver Spur. He used the door on to Main Street, nodding to the dudes as he passed; they were absorbed in a card game. He didn't think anyone would try violence while they were in town, but he crossed the width of the street quickly.

He kept in shadow as he walked towards the hotel. It was quite dark now.

Ray came running towards him, excited. 'I met Miss Ella — she runs the town paper and wants to meet yuh in the morning, to get all the details about the marshal's killing and everything.'

'Fine,' Toby said absently, his attention all on the street.

When they reached the hotel, Ray ran up the stairs, calling, 'I'll be in bed before you!'

Not likely, Toby thought with a smile; the door was locked. He reached for his key on the rack, but it wasn't there.

He went upstairs quickly. Ray was just opening the door, and Toby felt a draught from the window and shouted, 'Get down, Ray, get down!'

The boy didn't hesitate, but flung himself headlong to the floor.

Toby could smell . . . what was that smell? He sniffed the air as an indistinct figure moved towards him. It stumbled over Ray and muttered a curse. A missile whistled past Toby's ear and embedded itself in the wall with a thud. Something quivered.

In the dark, he made a wild grab and clutched at a shirt. The material tore, and his attacker retreated to the window and leapt through.

'Are you all right, Ray?'

'Sure.' Ray pulled his knife from its sheath. 'Has he gone?'

Toby crossed to the window and peered out; the street was in shadow and he saw no one, but heard running footsteps that faded quickly with distance.

'He's gone.'

Toby lit the lamp and looked around; nothing appeared to have been disturbed. They had not interrupted a robbery; his bag had not even been opened.

Someone knew who he was and why he was here. Whoever it was just wanted to get rid of him, to stop him asking questions. He smiled, sure he was on the right trail at last.

Ray pulled the missile out of the woodwork. 'It's an arrow.'

Toby looked it over with some interest, and corrected, 'Arrowhead. There are no flight-feathers — just enough shaft to grip in the hand.'

Ray was excited. 'Indians?'

'That smell was bear-grease,' Toby said, 'and some Indians use it.' As Ray's eyes widened, he added, 'I guess someone really wants us to think it was an Indian who attacked us.'

6

The Crooked L

Toby was eating breakfast with Ray — bacon, beans, hash-browns and coffee — when the newspaper owner arrived at the dining-room.

She looked around, made straight for Ray, and sat down. 'You must be Toby.'

He smiled pleasantly. ''Morning, Miss Ella. Yes, Ray's been singing your praises, and I can see why.'

The owner stepped from behind the counter with a mug of coffee and Ella said, 'Thanks, Cookie.'

She got out a pad and pencil. This morning, her face was newly scrubbed and she wore old jeans, a man's shirt and unpolished riding boots.

'Name,' she said briskly.

'Toby Small. I don't know a lot more than Ray told yuh, yet, but I aim to find

51

out. No one knew the dead man was a federal marshal until later. He'd been shot in the back, twice.'

He waited for her pencil to pause before continuing: 'My brother, George — who never could mind his own business — picked up the gun and the sheriff arrested him. I know my brother couldn't kill anyone, so I'm asking around, trying to find the real killer.'

'Great story,' she said. 'But will anyone else believe your brother innocent?'

Ray burst out, 'Someone tried to kill us last night. In the dark, in our hotel room — with an arrowhead!'

'An arrowhead? Are you saying we have hostiles around?'

Toby shrugged. 'Whoever it was got away.'

Ella regarded him steadily. Her friendliness seemed at an end; her voice grew chilly.

'Maybe it's not safe for Ray to be with you. Maybe you should send him home. Or are you just out to make trouble?'

Toby smiled. 'I early formed a habit of avoiding trouble.'

'So why are you in Tumbleweed?'

'Just asking questions.'

'It could be you won't be popular,' she said. 'We don't want our paying visitors disturbed in any way. The whole town depends on them coming here and spending money — so we look after them.'

'I'm looking after my brother, and I don't aim to let him hang for a crime he didn't commit. Or let the real killer get away with it.'

'But why look here?'

'When I asked here, I got a reaction. Somebody in Tumbleweed knows something.'

'I'll run the story because it's news,' she said abruptly, and stood up. 'But if you can take a tip, you'll clear off before Marshal Lee hears you're stirring things up . . . and you, Ray, you'd best go home.'

As she moved briskly towards the door, Toby called out, 'Who gives your marshal his orders?'

The door banged behind her, and Cookie laughed.

'Sure feel sorry for the man who marries that one — but she's right about the town getting nasty if you spoil it for the dudes.'

Cookie came from behind the counter to collect the dirty plates and mugs, and Toby saw he had a lame leg.

'But not you?'

He shrugged. 'Dudes don't come here. If they eat in town, it's at the hotel. Mac's store does all right with fancy duds. The saloons take money, and they don't seem to mind losing at cards. It's a game to them — but a living to Tumbleweed folk.

'And it's Harknett who gives Lee his orders . . . '

★ ★ ★

Ella crossed to the livery stable, saddled her horse and rode out of town, taking the track that led to the Crooked L.

54

Small's story disturbed her and she wasn't sure why. She wasn't used to feeling doubt.

Ella considered herself a practical young lady, confident and independent. She had charge of her own life and intended to go her own way.

But she liked the boy, Ray, and thought he might be in danger. Small annoyed her; it was easy to see what he was and she disapproved.

The trail wound between hills barely covered by short, burned grass. It was rocky country where not much grew; a wilderness compared to some parts she'd visited. It was why the Crooked L ranch had failed until Harknett got the idea of bringing in wealthy Easterners. Between them they had saved the ranch and Tumbleweed too.

But the murder of a United States marshal was news, and she hadn't heard a whisper of it until now. Carver made regular visits, the marshal must be in touch with the county sheriff. Ella didn't like it. As a newspaper woman, the smell of secrecy made her suspicious. What of, she wasn't sure — but she intended to find out.

She saw, as she neared the ranch, that Harknett had spent money to make the place comfortable for the dudes, and wondered where he'd got it. She rode down to the house and called, 'Anyone home?'

The rancher stepped outside.

'Ella, this is a pleasant surprise.' He had a Southern drawl and a courteous manner. 'Set down and come inside. I'll fix coffee.'

She turned her horse loose to graze in the corral, walked up the steps to the veranda and into the cool. She knew he was keen on her and she kept a certain distance between them. There was a weakness there and she'd been brought up on the frontier to respect those who survived. And any form of weakness was not a survival trait.

She sat down when he brought coffee; cup and saucer, Eastern style, she noted.

'Thanks . . . it's information, I'm after. There's a stranger in Tumbleweed telling a story about a murdered marshal . . . '

Harknett smiled faintly. 'I've heard something along those lines from my foreman.'

'I've got to put something in my paper because, obviously, it's news. But this man — Small — reckons he's hunting for the killer to save his brother. And he's here.'

Harknett looked unhappy. 'I'll get Carver — I know he's around somewhere.' He went to the door and called out. Minutes later the foreman came in.

'Yes, boss? Hi, Miss Ella.'

Sometimes she thought he was interested in her, but his unwinking stare put her off. Apart from that he was as handsome as any man she'd met.

'Ella reports a man named Small is in Tumbleweed and — '

'Yeah, saw him in the Silver Spur. Somehow he got the drop on Blackie. I haven't figured him yet — he could be trouble.'

'Trouble is the last thing we need, Carver. We must allow nothing to alarm our guests.' The rancher turned to Ella. 'I suggest you play down this murder story until all the facts are available.'

Carver stared coldly at her, eyes shielded by the brim of his hat. 'The only fact that needs reporting is that Sheriff Nash has the murderer safely in jail waiting for the judge.'

Ella protested, 'But his brother — '

'That's it, Miss Ella.' Carver's lips made a smile as cold as his stare. '*His brother*. You can see why he'd like to pin it on somebody else, anybody else.'

'Exactly,' Harknett said, nodding. 'We must leave it to the judge, Ella. We all depend on our friends from the East — even you. Nothing unpleasant must disturb their visits.'

She frowned. 'This Small also claims he was attacked in his hotel bedroom.'

Carver laughed. 'That *hombre* sure has got imagination!'

'He also has a witness, a boy who's travelling with him. I believe there was an attack. He mentioned an arrow-head.'

'Indians now?' Harknett commented, amused. 'Come on, Ella, I accept you want something sensational for your paper, but you can't possibly take such nonsense seriously.'

'Perhaps not,' she conceded, 'but I didn't ride out just to talk about this stranger. I got the idea to write up the Crooked L — it would make an interesting piece for local people, and give you a bit of publicity. I know folk who send the *Trumpet* back East to relatives, so you'd get some free advertising.'

Carver and Harknett glanced at each other. There was a brief silence, then the rancher said, in a strained voice, 'I think not, Ella. It's nice of you to offer, but we're not equipped to handle a sudden rush of clients. We get all the guests we need through personal contacts, and it takes more organizing than you might guess to cope with those we have. No, I thank yuh, but we must decline the offer.'

She saw Carver watching her with his reptilian eyes, and shivered. 'Whatever you say, Mr Harknett.'

She finished her coffee and went outside, collected her horse and rode away. Her back itched, and she knew both men were watching her.

She wondered what the hell was going on.

★ ★ ★

The largest general store in Snake City was not busy and Jackson sat in his own private corner with a pencil and account book, keeping an eye on his new assistant. His mind was not on his accounts, which showed a profit; and he never worried beyond that.

Jackson was approaching middle age, and his mind often wandered. The town was growing, his store was growing with it and, every now and again, he realized he needed a son to continue the business in his name. He was considering taking a wife.

Naturally he thought of Polly Small, soon to be made a widow. He found her attractive and her husband had boasted of her cooking. She was wasted on George, of course, who would never rise above the position of assistant.

In fact, he would soon find a new position as the hangman's assistant, and rise as far as he ever would in this world. Jackson shook with suppressed laughter at his little joke.

It was time, he decided, to make his move, before others with a roving eye starting courting her. An offer of help now would bring him to her attention in the nicest possible way.

Of course, she was pregnant; any fool could see that. But that only proved she could give him the son he wanted.

When Polly came into the store he was on his feet immediately, pushing past his assistant.

'Mrs Small, I hope you're managing

during this difficult time. It's occurred to me that I might be able to help by providing some modest credit, say up to twenty dollars until . . . '

There was no point in mentioning this was the amount in cash Toby had given him for that purpose.

' . . . well, until things are settled.'

Polly seemed embarrassed, then relieved. 'That would be helpful, Mr Jackson. Toby offered, but he's out of town and I find myself a bit short.'

Jackson beamed. 'I'm glad I can help, my dear. For you, anything . . . '

7

The Photographer's Daughter

'Look,' Ray said, excited. 'There's one of them dudes!'

Toby glanced along Main Street towards the editorial office of the *Tumbleweed Trumpet*; it was noticeably quiet without the press clanking away. He saw a tall man dressed like a cowboy standing stiffly erect on the boardwalk outside the office.

'Sure ain't no cowpuncher,' he agreed, noting the brand-new gear the man was wearing: wide-brimmed Stetson, leather gunbelt and holstered revolver and spurs that jingled when he moved.

They ambled along for a close look. The visitor's face was red where the sun had caught him and he seemed self-conscious, as if dressed for a party.

Ray said, 'If you're waiting for Miss Ella, she's gone a-riding. Saw her get her horse a while back.'

The dude frowned. 'But I had an appointment for a photograph!'

Toby smiled and drawled, 'Maybe meeting times ain't quite as rigid in Tumbleweed as those back East. Guess she'll be along later.'

'And I thought she was a businesswoman.'

'Can't argue with that,' Toby said.

'It's for my people back home. I have to show I was really out West, you know.'

'Sure,' Toby agreed. 'Fancy a game of cards to pass the time?'

The Easterner brightened. 'Good idea — let's go to the Silver Spur. My name's Ambrose.'

'Toby. I want yuh to wait here, Ray, and let us know when Miss Ella gets back.'

They walked along to the saloon, where it was obvious Ambrose was well known. He called for brandy.

Toby drawled, 'Not for me, friend. I never drink when I'm playing for money — I like to keep a clear head.'

Ambrose got a new pack of cards from behind the counter, and a couple of townsmen joined them.

'The game is blackjack,' Toby said. 'I'm against gambling, and this is a game of skill.'

Ambrose was invited to deal first; he dealt two cards to each player, face down.

Toby looked at his pair and called, 'Buy one.' Ambrose dealt him a card face down. Toby picked it up, glanced at it and said, 'Stick.'

He made twenty-one first and collected the pot. He continued to demonstrate his skill by winning most of the hands; and, as they played, he dropped in casual questions about the Crooked L ranch.

'It's an experience,' Ambrose said. 'We have to rough it a bit, but that's part of the fun. I'm from Boston, my first trip West — and it won't be the last. I'll have a few stories to tell when I get back.'

'How d'yuh figure the boss? And the foreman?'

'Mr Harknett's a gentleman, easy to get along with. Carver, I rather fancy, could turn nasty if anyone upset him.'

'When you came through Snake City, did you — '

A sharp voice came from behind Toby. 'I thought I warned you off, Small. And now I catch you cheating at cards.'

Ambrose looked up with a surprised expression. 'I don't think so, Mr Lee. I have enough card sense to know that much — and we're only playing for small stakes.'

The town marshal seemed taken aback. 'I'm watching yuh, feller, and this is my last warning. Another wrong move and you're in jail. We don't need any light-fingered gents in Tumbleweed.'

Toby smiled easily. 'Take a seat, Marshal, and I'll explain the game.

Anyway, I expect to spend my winnings in your town.'

As the game continued, Toby said patiently, 'Blackjack is a matter of memory and calculating odds that change all the time.'

'When you see the ten-cards played, you know the pack is ten-poor and that changes the odds — so you need to keep a running count in your head of the proportion of high to low cards.'

'So you say,' Lee muttered.

As they kept playing, Toby stayed that bit ahead until Ray stuck his head over the batwings and announced, 'Miss Ella's back.'

Ambrose finished the hand and stood up. 'Thank you, gentlemen. I have an appointment now, but I'll be glad to join you in a game another time.'

Toby pocketed his winnings and followed the dude outside. He had an idea where Ella might have gone and wanted to ask a couple of questions.

Ray walked alongside the dude, clearly fascinated by him. Toby strolled behind. Large prints of forests and mountains and plains covered the studio walls.

Ella, he noted, had found time to change into a smart dress to meet Ambrose. Yes, he thought, she's a businesswoman all right.

Ambrose was obviously impressed, but Ray didn't seem to like the change. Toby stayed in the background, near the door, to observe.

The camera, part wooden box and part bellows, was mounted on a tripod. Ella placed Ambrose against a white cloth to get maximum reflection of light from the door and window.

'The exposure time is approximately one minute,' she said crisply. 'For that minute, Mr Ambrose, I must ask you to remain perfectly still. Try to relax. Imagine you're a cowhand at the end of a trail drive — you're happy to hit town, have a decent meal, get a few drinks and a bath . . . '

She ducked her head under a dark cloth. 'Quite still, please . . . good.' She removed the lens cap. 'Hold that . . . right, all over! Thank you.'

She took the glass plate from the camera and moved swiftly into another room, closing the door behind her. Toby smelt chemicals.

When Ella came out again, she said, 'It's a good one, developed nicely. I'll make prints later.'

Ambrose beamed. 'That's fine — I'd like six copies, please. It would be even better if you'd have dinner with me tonight. I thought, at the hotel.'

She nodded. 'Of course. I'll join you in the hotel dining-room about eight.'

The dude left with a jaunty air, but Ray turned on her with a scornful look.

'Why d'yuh say that? You can do things — run a newspaper, take pictures. You don't have to run after some Eastern dude playing at cowboys. I'd expect that from my sister . . . '

'You and Toby now — he does interesting things too . . . '

Ella raised an eyebrow and looked at Toby. He said, quickly, 'Ray, please go and check on Millie and Monty.'

Ray sniffed and walked out.

Ella said easily, 'All the dudes ask me to dinner. There are only so many unattached women in Tumbleweed.'

'I'd ask you myself,' Toby said, 'if I thought you'd accept.' He indicated the pictures on the wall. 'Yours? I'm impressed.'

'My father's — and so you should be. He was a pioneer. He carried all his equipment — wet plates, chemicals, dark-room tent on a packhorse — and travelled right across this country. Running a studio is nothing compared to that.'

Toby smiled. 'I have to agree with Ray about that. What happened at the Crooked L?'

Her face clouded. 'I don't know what to make of it. Both Mr Harknett and Carver knew about the marshal. Neither had thought to say anything to me, and they tried to play down the attack on you. So as not to alarm our visitors, of course, which is not unreasonable.'

She paused. 'When I offered to run a piece on the ranch, I was turned down. They don't want publicity. I find that a bit odd, so what's going on?'

'When I find out, you'll be the first to hear — and I hope you'll print it.'

Her face flushed. 'If it's true, I'll print it — and be damned.'

'Fine,' Toby said, and left. Outside, he saw Lee across the road, watching him like a hawk about to pounce on its prey.

He briefly considered the idea of a night reconnaissance of the ranch and rejected it; he didn't know the lie of the land well enough.

He collected Ray and they went for their evening meal.

'It's steak with onions,' Cookie said, and chatted as he put the pan on the stove.

'You got an opinion of Mr Lee?' Toby asked.

'A nothing. You push him, he'll fall over.'

'How about the cowhands at the Crooked L?'

Cookie flicked long grey hair out of his eyes.

'Cowhands? Gunmen more like it. I worked as cook to cowhands on cattle drives till I broke my leg. No trail boss would take that crew on.'

They ate their steak and washed it down with strong black coffee.

'Bed, young Ray,' Toby said. 'I want to be away early in the morning.'

Immediately after breakfast he hitched Millie and Monty and, with Ray sitting beside him, set off to explore the immediate area.

Lee was up early too, watching, and Toby raised his hat and waved as they passed by. Ray, he thought, seemed unusually subdued.

The direct trail was well worn and easy enough to follow, but he didn't want to announce himself in advance. He left the trail and veered towards the hills, to approach by a roundabout route.

The country was mostly wilderness, bare hills and scrubby brush with an occasional stand of trees; the hills were split by canyons with naked rock faces. In the distance he heard water rushing over rocks and guessed that, not far away, a river had rapids.

The desolate area made him think about George, sitting alone in his cell, waiting for the judge to arrive . . .

★ ★ ★

Judge Benson began to wonder what was going on. He was not used to being kept waiting and his blood pressure was rising. He felt as if he had been waiting for hours with no explanation for the delay though, at most, it had been minutes.

He sat in the tiny school, used as a courthouse, at Three Corners, waiting. Impatiently.

Some of these small Western towns were real time-wasters, and he considered — as he had more than once before — whether they should be on his circuit at all.

Outside the children, given a day's holiday, were celebrating noisily.

He glowered at a deputy. 'Where is the accused? Why isn't he here?'

'He's a-coming, your Honour.'

Benson's black bar eyebrows lifted into question marks.

'Yes sir, Judge sir, he's — er . . . ' The deputy didn't know quite how to phrase his explanation, and resented being left to face the judge alone.

Benson was a powerful and threatening sight in his black robe. He had the rugged build of a statue carved from granite, and his name was borrowed by parents to subdue unruly offspring.

'It seems, your Honour, that the prisoner escaped — '

'Escaped!' The courtroom seemed to darken as Benson's frown deepened into a scowl.

'Yes, sir, escaped from jail, and the sheriff has taken a posse after him. When they catch him — '

'When!' Gimlet eyes bored into the deputy. 'When your sheriff returns, inform him that I have better things to do than wait on his incompetence.'

The judge rose abruptly and gathered his robe about him. 'I have an appointment in Snake City with the killer of a federal lawman, and shall allow no delay.'

As he stalked away, he snapped, 'I suggest you build a stronger jail, and vote in a new sheriff!'

8

The Escape

As the wagon came down from the hills, Toby saw the ranch in the valley and studied the layout. It may have been extensive at one time, but now he saw only a few head of cattle grazing and horses in a corral. The outbuildings were not in good repair, though the ranch house had obviously been smartened up.

Some distance away there appeared to be a box canyon with a stand of trees and tangled undergrowth; he guessed this was all that was left of what had been a wood in the past. It was almost certainly a dead end.

He could see someone sitting on the veranda of the house, and a bunch of men gathered about some cattle. He got out a pair of army binoculars — won in a card game — polished the lenses and

76

focused. Easterners, a couple of Crooked L men and Carver, the foreman. He identified Blackie and wondered whether he might smell of bear grease.

'I'm going down there, Ray, to ask a few questions. I don't expect trouble while the dudes are around but, just in case, stay here and keep out of sight.'

'I'll scout around a bit, and see what I can spot.'

'Right.'

Toby flicked the reins and Millie and Monty went forward again. Ray dropped off and disappeared into some brush.

Toby didn't hurry or attempt to hide his approach. When he got nearer, he saw the foreman was demonstrating branding to the dudes.

There was a small fire burning, and Carver held a long iron. As Toby drove nearer he could smell singed hair. A couple of men, one an Easterner, held down a calf.

Toby stopped a little way off and remained in his seat as men turned to look at him.

Carver frowned. 'You, Small. What the hell d'you want here?' He tugged down the brim of his hat to shield his eyes.

'Just dropped by to ask a couple of questions.'

Carver's face registered frustration. It was obvious he wanted to get rid of him, but the presence of the dudes prevented him from taking direct action.

'Quite simple questions,' Toby drawled. 'While you were in Snake City, did you see who gunned down the marshal? Or hear who did?' He glanced around the ring of faces. 'Questions apply to anyone who saw or heard anything.'

There was a general shaking of heads. A few more of Carver's men drifted up.

Only the dudes showed any interest and it began to seem this was the first time they'd heard about the murder — assuming they were telling the truth.

The Crooked L men said nothing, just looked at the foreman for orders. Each one struck Toby as a potential killer; they did not look like working cowhands; he got the idea he was lucky the Easterners were present.

He wondered why the rancher should want such an outfit; each one had the same stamp as Blackie.

Harknett came from the veranda of the house, taking long strides.

'What's going on here? Who is this man?'

'Name's Small,' Carver answered, not taking his gaze off Toby. 'Asking questions about a dead marshal in Snake City.'

Harknett glanced at him. 'I see.' He forced a smile and relaxed. When he spoke again, he had a Southern drawl. 'Providing you're only asking questions, Mr Small, there's no objection. However, any accusations . . . '

Toby said mildly, 'I'm not accusing anyone. Just trying to find out what happened. My brother's been arrested for it, and I'm sure he didn't pull the trigger.'

Harknett nodded. 'You're bound to

support your brother, that's only natural. But I suggest you leave it for the judge to decide — that's what the law is all about.'

One or two of the Easterners murmured approval.

Harkness tried a tougher line. 'I must, however, point out that this is private property and that you are trespassing.'

Carver hitched up his gunbelt, and one of the dudes warned, 'Perhaps you should leave, Mr Small. Mr Carver has demonstrated that he is, indeed, a fast and accurate shootist.'

Toby glanced over the paying guests. All smartly dressed in new cowpuncher's clothes, they were probably wealthy and capable back East. Here they would be no match for the Crooked L roughnecks.

The foreman laughed, a harsh sound. 'Yeah, and don't come back, feller.' He shoved the branding-iron in the fire to reheat and stood staring at Toby, his arrogant stance a challenge in itself.

There was something wrong about his eyes, Toby realized. He stared without blinking, the way a snake did. It was unnerving.

He looked away at the ring of faces. 'Guess I'll see some of you in town.'

Carver snatched the hot iron from the fire and came towards the wagon. 'If I catch yuh on Crooked L land again, I'll put our brand on yuh, the same as I would any stray steer.'

Harknett said quickly, for the benefit of the visitors, 'A joke. He's joking, of course.'

But Toby felt the scorching heat of the iron as he came close and knew the foreman meant what he threatened. He shook the reins and turned the mules and headed back towards Tumbleweed.

★　★　★

Ray felt great because now he could adventure on his own. Toby had agreed, more or less, that he should scout around. 'Keep out of sight,' he'd said.

Ray watched the wagon trundle away, then darted quickly towards long grass. He remembered the arrowhead in the hotel room; maybe there really were Indians about! He dropped to his knees and crawled through the grass, peering out now and then to get his bearings.

He headed for the canyon they'd seen earlier; that was a likely place to explore and, from one of the walls, he'd be able to look down and keep an eye on the wagon and Millie and Monty.

The mouth of the canyon was screened by spiky brush — yet he discovered faint trail leading into it. This was something to tell Toby — he was earning his keep — brush had been dragged across the entrance to hide it.

He moved some of the loose branches, just enough to wriggle through, wondering: why would anyone try to block a canyon?

Inside the valley stretched a long way back. It was not wide, but there were trees and bushes and dense scrub between high rock walls. Was there another way out? He would have to climb to see the ranch from here. He was looking for a way up when he spotted a log cabin among the trees.

It looked to be in liveable condition, and he assumed it belonged to the ranch, but why was it hidden away here? There was no-one about so he crept closer.

The window had boards nailed over it, and the door was barred — on the outside. Ray stared blankly. Nobody could get out. He walked quietly around the cabin, but there was no other door.

Then he heard a faint movement inside.

Ray froze, his heart pounding.

A weak voice came from inside.

'If there's anyone there, please help me.'

Ray edged his way silently to the window and tried to peer through a crack between the boards; he could see nothing but a grey gloom.

The voice came again. 'Help me,

please — I can reward you.'

Ray backed off, looking around him. He saw no-one else about. Who was it inside? This really was an adventure, though he began to wish Toby was here.

Then he remembered Ella. Not the dolled-up photographer who'd gone off to dinner with a dude, but the hard-working newspaperwoman with a hand press. There was a story here she would buy.

He tried the bar across the door. It was heavy, but farm work had built muscle and he could lift it. The door opened easily on oiled hinges.

The interior was bare apart from a bunk and a water jug on the floor beside it. A man lay on the bunk, blinking in the sudden light; he seemed dazed.

One end of a rope was tied around his neck, the other end around a beam in the room. He had just enough slack to reach the jug.

Ray drew his knife and cut the rope. Excitement surged through him. Why had the prisoner been shut in here? What had he done?

The man mumbled thanks and sipped from the jug. He tried to stand and almost fell.

'Got to get away. Help me.'

Obviously, he hadn't used his legs for a long time. The whiskers sprouting from his chin indicated that. Ray got an arm around the man and helped him to stagger outside. What now? The prisoner could only move slowly and was too weak to climb a rock wall.

Ray replaced the bar across the door. If he could hide the man somewhere, he'd fetch Toby. Together, they limped away towards the trees.

* * *

Millie and Monty seemed determined to drag their heels. They were obstinate about leaving, reluctant to step out faster than their slowest pace.

Toby swore at them. 'What's got into you two? C'mon, let's get out of here before Carver forgets himself and throws lead this way. Move!'

Millie brayed. Monty brayed. Neither showed any inclination to quicken their stride. The wagon lurched forward with painful slowness; it might reach Tumbleweed the day after tomorrow, Toby calculated.

'If it's young Ray you're missing, he's old enough to look after himself.'

Eventually the mules caught on that the boy wasn't coming back with them and began to trot along as if they'd remembered some tasty hay in the livery stable.

Toby brooded in the driving seat. He couldn't make up his mind about the Crooked L. On the face of it, Harknett was simply catering for Easterners who fancied a taste of Western living. Carver and his bunch told a different story. And why should the rancher get nervous about a casual visitor?

Maybe Ray would learn something useful. Adventurous boys often got where adults couldn't, and sharp young eyes could spot things he might miss. He'd wait till Ray got back before deciding his next move.

He worried about George. His brother's waiting time was getting shorter with every day; the judge might turn up at Snake City any time.

It was true George had always annoyed him with his righteous attitude and preaching, always going on about drinking and gambling and making an honest living. But he was still family and Toby had to get him out of the mess he'd got himself into. For Polly's sake.

His best chance, he concluded, still seemed to be to trace the real killer.

★ ★ ★

Whit Chancellor, owner of Snake City's bank, was a solid man who liked to think of himself as a solid citizen. He controlled money and that gave him a sense of power. He acknowledged he'd come a long way since his days as a carpetbagger after the war.

He dressed well, ate well and moved with the slow determination of the self-satisfied. He took a glass of brandy or smoked a cigar when he was in an expansive mood. He took trouble to meet people who could do him a favour.

He stood outside his bank, in the sun, smoking and watching the world go by. He liked to think of Snake City as his town. Occasionally he would nod to a customer, or frown as someone who owed money darted down an alley.

He saw Jackson escort a customer to his wagon, and his lip curled. Why couldn't the man wait until after the hanging?

Things were quiet, orderly, the way he liked them to be. And, obviously, the town was still growing, and he intended to prosper with it.

As he'd anticipated, the railroad made the difference. People with money were coming, wanting land — and he held a mortgage on more than one property. Land prices could only go up.

At one time he'd almost decided to go into politics, but changed his mind. Why bother when, with money, he could buy all the politicians he needed?

It seemed all was right in the world of Whit Chancellor, a strong upholder of law, order and decorum. Then he frowned. At first he doubted his eyes. He blinked rapidly and looked again. He was not mistaken.

George Small's widow-to-be was strolling along the boardwalk as bold as brass and arm-in-arm with the sheriff's wife. Of course, Anna Nash was German; but even so it showed ignorance of the social niceties.

He chucked his cigar in the dust and ground it under his heel; he never left a stub for someone less fortunate to finish. He called to his clerk:

'I shall be back in ten minutes, Silas.'

Then he strode along the boardwalk to talk to Sheriff Nash.

★ ★ ★

Harknett tried to relax with a tumbler of Southern Comfort after Small left. It seemed he needed whiskey as a prop more and more these days. He tried not to worry, but still one thing after another went wrong.

He sat in a wicker chair on the veranda, remembering better times in the old South, and stared without seeing over his range, dreaming of what might have been.

There was little left of his herd and the bank held a mortgage on the land. He hoped the Easterners would pay that off eventually. He'd hoped to marry Ella but that appeared unlikely. Now it seemed trouble was back in the person of Toby Small. He felt apprehensive about any stranger visiting.

When he heard hoofbeats, he shrugged off his mood. Carver was coming fast. More trouble. Harknett sighed and roused himself.

His foreman vaulted from his horse,

stepped up to the veranda and helped himself to whiskey.

Sometimes, Harknett thought, he acted as though he owned the place.

Carver wiped his mouth with the back of his hand. 'Wallace escaped.'

Harknett felt an icy hand clutch his heart. This was the worst yet.

'How the devil could he get out of that cabin?'

'Someone helped him. There's no other way. Someone outside let him out and then replaced the bar.'

'So now somebody else knows!'

'Yeah . . . I'm guessing. Remember we had a visit from Small? All our attention was on him then — '

'What can we do? If Wallace should talk to one of the Easterners . . . ' Harknett shuddered.

'I've sent them away. The whole group's riding the range, and I told Lefty to take them the long way round.'

'We must find Wallace — '

'I've already got men searching and I'm leaving to take charge. He can't have got far. I had to warn yuh in case the dudes get back first.'

'I'll take care of them. You catch Wallace and whoever helped him.'

Carver finished his drink, climbed back on his horse and rode away.

Harknett refilled his tumbler with a shaking hand.

If Wallace got away it was all over, finished. He cursed the day he'd ever believed this reckless scheme could solve his problems.

He gulped his drink and stood up. He moved well, smiling easily. It was business as usual and nobody would guess the desperation behind the mask. He practised his 'good old boy' act for when the Easterners returned.

9

In Hazard

Ray had continually to help the man he'd freed. He was unsteady on his feet and stumbled over tufts of grass, too weak to help himself. Ray had well developed muscles for his age but, even so, he found it hard going.

They got away from the immediate vicinity of the cabin, moving among trees and undergrowth, keeping inside the wood to use it as cover.

The unknown man gasped, 'I can't keep going much longer. And they'll be hunting me soon.'

'Try to hold out for a bit,' Ray urged. 'The further we get from that cabin the better.'

They struggled on till hoofbeats sounded among the brush and the prisoner said grimly, 'Here they come!'

'We'll dodge them,' Ray said confidently. 'Like this.' He led the way deeper into the brush. 'We'll lie low here. Heads down, and keep still and quiet.'

There came the sound of men and horses passing by, cursing. After a pause, a hard voice said, 'Spread out — make a wider search.'

The prisoner whispered, 'My name's Wallace, and I'm from the East. Get away and tell the sheriff I was held a prisoner at the cabin. Go now, while you can. I'll only hold you back.'

Ray didn't want to desert his new friend and left it late. The hunt came nearer. Men thrashed the bushes with cudgels, poking into the undergrowth with sharpened stakes. Ray pressed himself into the earth and slowed his breathing; he thought it was going to be all right, that the hunt was moving away.

Then one of them fired a revolver, shredding the leaves just above his head. It was the first time he'd been

94

under fire and he jumped.

'Here,' a voice shouted. 'I've flushed one of them!'

'Good work, Slim.'

Ray, desperate, made a run for it, to take their attention away from the prisoner. He was knocked flying by a charging horse, grabbed by his shirt and clubbed viciously with the barrel of a revolver. He dropped, blood running into his eyes.

'Got this one . . . jeez, it's only a kid!'

Men came tramping through the undergrowth, laying about with stakes.

'And here's Wallace . . . '

Carver arrived, gun in hand.

'Right. Tie their hands behind them. Tie their ankles but allow enough slack so they can walk back to the cabin.' He glared at them. 'More of this nonsense and I'll kill the pair of yuh.'

Ray's head ached, but when he looked into the foreman's eyes, he forgot about that. He shivered, convinced that Carver meant to kill him.

Hobbled, Ray and Wallace stumbled their way back to the cabin. They were roughly pushed inside.

Carver followed them in. 'Who are yuh, kid? How did yuh get here? Did Small send yuh?'

When Ray didn't answer, Carver grabbed hold of his ear and twisted savagely. Ray howled, his eyes watering.

'Answer me!' Carver laughed as tears streamed down his face. 'We'll see what the boss decides — I know what I'd do.' He jabbed Ray in the ribs with the muzzle of his revolver.

One of the men tied him to the bunk; another took his knife away.

Carver stepped outside and the door was barred.

'Luckily there's no harm done. So it's back to normal duties as soon as the dudes return. You, Guzman, stay on guard here. I'll see you're relieved later but, from now on, Wallace must be watched all the time.'

★ ★ ★

Toby shaved and breakfasted early, then sauntered along to the newspaper office. Ella had not yet arrived and the lock turned easily with a piece of stiff wire.

He looked over the press; he'd used one before and this appeared to be a standard model. Whistling cheerfully, he set the type he wanted, inked it and selected a suitable paper. He began to print, laying out the sheets to dry.

His work was going well when Ella stepped through the doorway.

'Just what d'you think you're doing? And how did you get in?'

Toby continued to run off printed copy.

''Morning, Miss Ella. Anyone can open your lock. And I'm printing labels — naturally, I'll pay for the paper.'

Ella picked up one of the sheets to read:

Dr Tobias's Universal Remedy
For chills, stomach pains and falling hair.
Also an excellent purge for the bowels

She frowned. 'So now you're some kind of horse doctor.'

'I have treated Millie and Monty, when necessary.'

He stopped printing. 'That's enough for the present. When I've stuck them on my bottles, I'll be in business. What do I owe you?'

'I'd charge anyone else a dollar. As you're some kind of cheap swindler, you'll pay double. What's in the bottles?'

Toby paid her. 'Alcohol, a few herbs, and my secret ingredient.'

'What's that?'

He smiled. 'If I told yuh, it wouldn't be a secret, would it? I'll give you a bottle.'

'No, thanks,' she said hastily. 'Where's Ray?'

'Doing what boys do best. Adventuring.'

'Where?'

'Somewhere around the Crooked L.'

'You left him out there?' She sounded disturbed. 'Alone?'

'Why not? Ray's all right — you needn't worry.'

'It's obvious you don't,' Ella said tartly. 'I don't trust Carver.'

Toby finally focused on her words, 'Why not? What d'yuh know about him? How come the ranch boss has a crew like that?'

'It's common knowledge he's a gunfighter. Most assume he's outside the law. Personally, I don't like the man and don't trust him. At one time, Mr Harknett had genuine cowhands, but had to let them go. Then Carver arrived — he was the one who hired the present crew.'

Toby considered this information. It irritated him to realize it must mean something, but he couldn't think what. After all, he was only concerned about George.

Ella turned away with a disgusted expression. 'I'm going to find Ray.'

He watched her cross the street to the livery stable. She brought out her horse, swung into the saddle and rode out of town.

Toby shrugged, then walked down

the street to Mac's Store. Like most buildings in Tumbleweed it had been spruced up; inside it was well stocked with riding-boots and Stetsons and fancy shirts. Fancy prices too, Toby noted.

'Help you?' Mac offered, watching closely. He had the appearance of having shrivelled with age.

Behind the counter he kept a supply of revolvers, rifles and boxes of ammunition.

'Just looking. I'll have to stock up before I leave town.'

Mac nodded. 'Got most things a travelling man needs — coffee, sugar, salt, beans, flour, tobacco.'

Toby said, 'Guess you do well out of the Crooked L visitors.'

'Well enough. Most folks here do.' Mac paused, looking towards the doorway. Marshal Lee stood there. 'That's why strangers likely to make trouble ain't popular. You let me know when you're moving on, and I'll stock you up real quick.'

Harknett paced the veranda of the Crooked L ranch house, furious. He felt a prisoner on his own land, yet he had to stay in case the Easterners returned. It had been, he now realized, a mistake to allow Carver so much authority; he could feel the reins slipping through his hands.

But with so much almost within his grasp he mustn't weaken; anything was better than the ruins in the South after the war. He still felt he'd had no choice, that he'd had to move his cattle and men north.

He stared across barren rangeland, unseeing. The dudes were not back yet so there was still a chance.

He heard distant hoofbeats and watched the rider; it was Carver coming at an easy lope and he assumed the worst was over. Relief flooded through him and he breathed easier.

When his foreman arrived, Harknett was smiling. Carver stepped down from his horse and climbed the steps to the veranda.

'Wallace is back in his cage. And we've got the boy who freed him.'

'Boy? What boy?'

Carver helped himself to the boss's Southern Comfort, and swallowed.

'Remember Small? When Van laid for him in the hotel, he said he tripped over a boy and had to run for it.'

'This boy is with Small?' Harknett felt uneasy. 'I'll question him myself. I want to know who he is, and what he's doing here.'

He avoided Carver's gaze.

'Send someone into town. Tell Lee to move Small on. We can't have him talking to our visitors again.'

⋆   ⋆   ⋆

Ella rode tight-lipped, furious with Toby. How could he leave a young boy out on the range alone? The man simply had no sense of responsibility.

She dug her spurs into her horse,

wishing it were Toby Small under her, and set a direct course for the Crooked L. After a while she realized she had allowed her disapproval of Toby to affect her judgement; she slowed down and started to keep a lookout.

So far she had seen no sign of life anywhere on the parched grassland. The plain swept away to a line of hills and it occurred to her that she had no real idea of where to start searching. She was reluctant to ask at the ranch, except as a last resort.

The sky was a vast dome of blue without even a bird in sight, but that didn't worry her. She had the blood of pioneers in her veins.

She glanced towards the box canyon, doubtful that anyone had been inside for years, but it might be just the place to attract an adventurous youngster. She turned her horse to make for it.

As she approached the mouth of the canyon, a rider came out and she recognized Carver. What was he doing there?

The Crooked L foreman spotted her at the same time and changed course to meet her. He reined back and stared into her face.

''Day, Miss Ella. You looking for the boss?'

She quietened her racing pulse. She didn't have to fear this man; he was a hired hand and a word to Harknett would put him in his place. But, a small voice nagged, the two of them were out here alone.

'I'm looking for young Ray. A boy who was travelling with Toby Small.'

'So that's his name. We caught him snooping where he shouldn't be. The boss is questioning him now.'

'He's all right then?'

'Sure. Feller who caught him clouted him one, but that's nothing.'

Was he mocking her? The eyes under the flat-crowned hat stared unwinkingly at her. Snake's eyes, cold-blooded and chilling.

He smiled, as if reading her thoughts. 'The boy's at the old cabin. If you follow me, I'll show yuh.'

He turned his horse and rode back towards the canyon. After a brief hesitation, Ella followed.

They skirted thorny brush and presently she saw a log cabin set among trees. One of Carver's men, armed, sat on a stump outside.

'The boy's inside,' Carver drawled.

Ella dismounted, pushed open the door and walked in.

10

Black Mask

Ella paused just inside the door; the interior was gloomy and she gave her eyes time to adjust. Then she saw Ray, his hands tied behind him, his ankles hobbled.

Harknett gripped him by the shoulders and was shaking him furiously.

'What's going on here?' she demanded.

Ray turned his head and shouted, 'Get away quick, Miss Ella!'

She glimpsed a man on a bunk, a rope around his neck. 'Who . . . ?'

Harknett seemed to go into shock when he saw her. She swung around, suddenly appreciating that this was not the time for questions — but the Crooked L foreman stood blocking the doorway.

He drawled, 'Guess we can't let yuh

print all the news, Miss Ella.'

She looked at Harknett, who appeared to have got over his shock. His face registered anger as he turned on Carver.

'You fool! Why did you have to bring her here?'

Carver shrugged carelessly. 'Said she was looking for the kid. His name's Ray, and he's travelling with Small.'

Harknett stared at her with a wild look, almost of despair. 'I'm sorry, Ella — you shouldn't have seen any of this.'

She said crisply, 'You have some explaining to do, Mr Harknett. *Trumpet* readers will want to know everything.'

The rancher remained silent, and Ella looked around the cabin; with the windows boarded over, bare of even a table or chair, it was more of a prison than a place to live.

Carver gave a laugh that was more like a bark.

'She and the boy must die, that's obvious.' He drew his revolver. 'I'll attend to it.'

Harknett shouted in an agonized

voice, 'No, not Ella!'

'You're a fool,' Carver said. 'Fancy her, do yuh? Think she'll keep her mouth shut? There's only one way to be sure.'

'If you dare . . . ' The rancher's voice was suddenly hard. 'I'm in charge here, and I'll decide what happens. She will stay at the ranch with me. Ella, you must give me your word that you won't talk to anyone about this.'

She looked calmly at him.

'And if I don't?'

There was a moment's silence. Harknett and Carver glowered at each other. Before either could answer, a man stepped through the doorway.

He was a solidly built black man wearing a city suit, his face was hidden by a black mask. Ella stared blankly.

'Quarrelling?' the newcomer asked. 'I came to find out what the hold-up is with our friend.' He gestured at the man on the bunk. 'Who is this woman? Who is the boy? What are they doing here?'

Carver's voice changed; it became smoother, quieter, more careful. Ella guessed the man in the mask was the one who counted here.

'The boy, Ray, is with Toby Small. We caught him trying to get our friend away from here. The woman runs a newspaper in Tumbleweed — '

Harknett interrupted: 'I'll vouch for Ella. She'll keep quiet.'

Black Mask turned to look at him. His voice carried authority; a man used to giving orders.

'Only a fool gets involved with a woman when money is concerned. I've heard of Small, asking questions, interfering — I've said before, there must be nothing to link us with Beaumont.'

He swung about to face Carver again. 'Put that gun away — I don't want any more busybodies sticking their noses into my business.'

He glanced casually at Ella and Ray. 'Their deaths must look like an accident. See to it.'

'If you say so,' Harknett mumbled, looking sick. 'I'm sorry, Ella.'

'I do say so,' the masked man said curtly.

Carver grinned. 'I know just the place.'

Black Mask nodded. 'Toby Small will be no trouble once the judge arrives. Any danger will be over then.'

He turned back to Harknett, and now his voice had a chill that might have come off the Arctic ice-cap. 'I came about Wallace — so tell me what you're doing about him.'

There was a brief silence before Harknett admitted, in a strained voice, 'He's being stubborn.'

'Stubborn? Are you going soft?'

Carver spoke up eagerly. 'I know an old rustler's trick . . . '

* * *

Toby had sold a few bottles of his Universal Remedy as he went from door to door in Tumbleweed when he saw trouble coming. Trouble in the form of a heavily built muscular man approaching with deliberate strides. He wore thick-soled boots and a lumber-jack's shirt.

'You,' he said to Toby, flexing ham-sized hands. 'I'm goin' to wrap your legs around your neck kinda permanent like. We don't want your sort selling our women rubbish and asking questions. Time you pulled stakes and lit out for the horizon.'

He paused, assumed a wrestler's crouch, and advanced with both arms outstretched.

Toby faced him, smiling, waiting. He caught the man by his wrists as he rushed forward to grapple, and fell backwards to the ground. Toby's feet came up, lodged in his attacker's stomach and assisted his flight over his head. Toby released his grip and the big man continued through the air to crash, head first, into a horse-trough. He lay there, dazed, all the fight knocked out of him.

Toby got to his feet and brushed the dust of Main Street from his coat. He saw Marshal Lee hurrying towards him.

The lawman's badge gleamed in the sun and Toby wondered if he'd polished it specially. For a moment he was reminded of George.

'G'day, Marshal,' he said smoothly. 'Just the man — I want to lay a complaint against this man. He made an unprovoked attack on me.'

'You can forget that bluff,' Lee said abruptly. 'I want you out of town. I'm giving yuh one hour.'

Toby raised an eyebrow.

'If you're still here after that, I'll sling yuh in the jail and lose the key. You'll stay there till yuh rot.'

'Not an attractive prospect, Marshal. One hour. I guess I'll have time to pack. Now, I have here a small bottle of — '

'Git!'

Toby made an elaborate pretence of consulting his watch.

'You do realize you're depriving the

good citizens of your town of my services?'

When the marshal didn't bother to reply, Toby sighed, walked to his hotel and climbed the stairs. He began to pack. From the window he saw Lee talking to the man who had attacked him.

Toby was used to being moved on, but never before had he been told to quit in such a short time. Twenty-four hours, yes. Somebody was reacting.

Thoughtful, he carried his bag down to reception and settled his bill. At the stable, he hitched Millie and Monty and drove his wagon out on to Main Street. He raised his hat to the marshal as he passed by and headed out of town.

After leaving the town limits, he circled round and made for the Crooked L ranch. That was where he'd left Ray and where Ella had rushed off to. Maybe one or the other had stirred up whoever gave Lee his orders. Harknett?

He took his time, letting the mules

set their own pace. The air was heating up, with little shade, and there was no hurry.

Suddenly the mules slowed to a stop, their ears pointing forward.

'So what are yuh seeing?' Toby asked quietly.

He shaded his eyes and squinted. In the distance he watched riders crossing the track at an angle. He got out his binoculars and focused.

He recognized Ray and Ella, surrounded by armed men. Alarm bells rang in his head as they headed for the hills.

'Move along now,' he told his friends, and settled to follow at a discreet distance.

The riders were climbing towards the top of a canyon. He couldn't follow them up there without being seen; but below were trees and brush and he guided the wagon in among them.

He knew he was approaching water; he could hear it rushing over stones.

'Wait,' he told Millie and Monty, and

continued on foot, keeping under a canopy of leaves.

He came out in a narrow canyon where water poured through in a flood. The rock walls were high and bare. In the water, he saw a line of rocks and white foam and heard the river roar as it dropped away. Rapids. Dark jagged rocks stuck up like hungry teeth at the edge of the drop.

He looked up to the top of the canyon, puzzled. Then he spotted a figure recognizable by his flat-crowned hat: Carver. So the others must be Crooked L men.

He watched as Ray and Ella were untied and dragged to the brink of the canyon. Ray struggled futilely. Ella appeared calm.

They threw Ray over first, then Ella. Two frail human bodies fell headlong into the canyon and the raging torrent below.

Toby stared, appalled.

★ ★ ★

George Small thought he was going mad. He couldn't understand why he was still locked in a cell in the Snake City jail. His brother, Toby, seemed to have disappeared — at least, Polly claimed she didn't know where he was. She still brought his meals, but didn't have much to say to him.

The deputy in charge today — the fat one — was right out of sympathy.

'We all know what Toby is, so forget him. He ain't coming back.'

George frowned. 'I demand to see the sheriff.'

'Owen's outa town, so I'm stuck with yuh. Anything else before I snatch forty winks?'

'Will you ask Mr Jackson to visit me? I want to be sure I'll get my old job back.'

'Don't figure Jackson'll want to see yuh, right now.' The deputy smirked. 'Besides, where you're going, work'll be assigned.'

'I'm not getting enough exercise in here.'

'Legs sure work good, the pacing you

116

do. Reckon you won't need a lot of muscle to play a harp — that's if you're as innocent as you make out. Want to see your Maker, don't yuh? Can't you get it through your head, we're all tired of hearing that old sad song.'

George rubbed a hand over the bristles on his jaw. There was a wild light in his eyes. 'I need a shave. Can you get me — '

The deputy was alarmed.

'None of that now! Stick it out till the judge gets here — don't want to disappoint everyone, do we? You'll get a good turn-out. The whole town's looking forward to the great day — why, some of the youngsters haven't ever seen a good hanging. Wouldn't surprise me if the mayor declared a public holiday!'

11

White Water

Toby stared as if paralysed as two bodies disappeared beneath the churning surface of the river. His brain was numb with shock; he was watching murder being done. Murder to look like an accident, that's why they had been freed at the last moment.

Neither Ray nor Ella could survive the maelstrom at the bottom of the rapids — he didn't even know if either could swim.

Seconds passed so slowly that time seemed to have come to a standstill. Toby stopped breathing. Then Ella's head bobbed above the water, her face pale as a skull, eyes like black pebbles gazing at him with an intensity that shocked him into action. *Do something!*

There was still an outside chance and he turned and ran for his wagon. He ran faster than he'd ever run before, grabbed a lariat and ran back to the canyon. He made a wide loop in one end and prayed he'd be in time.

A rocky path beside the river, hardly more than a ledge, had been cleared at some time for the portage of canoes. The ground was slippery from spray and he moved cautiously towards the falls. He didn't think he could be seen from above, assuming Carver and his crew were still up there. That was a chance he had to take.

He reached a point level with the foaming crest of the rapids and saw two dark heads, close together, among the white. Ella had one arm around the youngster, supporting him, while she clung to a rock with the other. Water swirled over and around them, trying to dislodge them; if she relaxed her grip for an instant, they would be swept over the brink.

Toby tied the end of the rope to a

stump of tree growing at the base of the canyon wall and tugged on it with all his strength. The stump held.

He separated the coils of his lariat and cast the loop. Driving spray ruined his throw and the noose fell in the water well short of his target. He retrieved the rope and cast again; this time the loop was carried towards the rock where Ella clung, and she struggled to get it over Ray's head and shoulders.

She signalled to Toby as she lost her grip on the rock and a surge took them both to the brink. He took the strain, winding the slack about the tree stump. The current tore at them but the rope held. Both Ella and Ray were slammed against sharp rocks as he hauled them closer to the side.

Ella gripped the rope with one hand, supporting the boy's head above the surface with the other. The roar of water was like a never-ending roll of thunder, drowning out all other sounds.

She swam with her legs to help them towards the safety of the path as slowly, gradually, Toby hauled them in. His arms ached; his legs, braced to take the strain, felt as if the muscles had locked.

Eventually he brought Ray close enough to get a hand to his arm and drag him ashore, barely conscious and bleeding from a cut in his forehead.

Ella still clung to the rope, and he got both arms around her and heaved her out of the spray; she floundered on the bank, exhausted and gasping, streaming water, her face and arms bruised.

Toby crouched over the boy, pumping water from his lungs till he struggled to sit up. Then he too rested. They stared at the white water for long minutes, contemplating that endless fall and what might have been.

Ray recovered first.

'That was something like an adventure!'

Ella squeezed water from her hair. She looked mad enough to tackle a grizzly, muttering, 'Figure to collect my uncle's rifle and go a-hunting that bastard, Carver!'

Toby coiled up his rope and they squelched back to the wagon, the sun drying their clothes on them.

It was a near silent trip back to Tumbleweed. Ella was outwardly calm but fuming inside and, by the time they reached town, the day was cooling and shadows lengthening.

Toby stopped at the livery stable.

'I suggest we change and get a meal and then talk things over.'

As he headed for Mac's store to get Ray new clothes, Ella said, 'There's something I have to do first,' and stalked towards the marshal's office.

'Let her go,' Toby murmured. 'She's all grown up.'

Ella stormed into the marshal's office, looking like a drowned rat whose fur had shrunk as it dried out. Her hair was awry, her expression grim.

'Miss Ella,' Lee said, startled, coming to his feet. 'What on earth's happened?'

'Not on earth. In the river.'

As she told her story, the marshal sat down. His expression became blank.

'That's attempted murder,' she finished, 'and you're the law around here. Are you going to arrest Carver and Harknett?'

Lee shrugged. 'It's outside my jurisdiction. I only work in town.'

Ella exploded. 'Some lawman! Harknett appointed you, so you won't go up against him — not even for a would-be murder.'

Lee flushed, but remained calm.

'You'll find a lot of people in Tumbleweed will take the same attitude. We all depend on the Crooked L and the dudes they bring West. Without them we'd be in trouble.'

'And so will Harknett when I've run off a special edition of the *Trumpet*. I'm not keeping quiet — and I'll be sending a copy to the sheriff — think about that, Marshal!'

As she stalked out, Lee's expression indicated that he was, indeed, thinking about her threat.

Ella changed into fresh clothes, brushed her hair and joined Toby and Ray in Cookie's dining-room. All three ate hungrily and in silence, then walked along to her office.

Ella brought out a rifle and loaded it.

'My uncle was a frontiersman and this is his. He taught me to shoot.'

She looked at Toby and her lips moved, as if she had trouble getting the words out. She tried again.

'All right, Mr Small — Toby — I was wrong about you. You saved Ray's life, and mine.'

Toby relaxed. It was an embarrassing moment but at least she wasn't going to burst into tears. She was more likely, he thought, to shoot somebody.

Ray said, impatiently, 'What are we going to do now?'

'Waal, to start with,' Toby said, 'you can tell me what you two did to make Carver take such drastic action.'

'Not just Carver. Harknett was in on it — '

'And the man in the black mask,' Ray burst out. 'I bet he's the boss!'

Ella made coffee and they sat in her tiny office trying to ignore the smell of ink. Between them, Ray and Ella told him about the prisoner in the cabin.

Toby listened in amazement. Did this have anything to do with a dead marshal in Snake City? He was worried about George; time was running out for his brother and he seemed only to be getting deeper into a mystery beyond his grasp.

'It was the masked man who gave the orders,' Ella said. 'Both Harknett and Carver obeyed him. So who is he?'

'And what do we do about it?' Toby murmured.

Ray, at least, had no doubts. 'We ought to rescue Mr Wallace — I bet he knows what's going on.'

Ella exchanged a wry look with Toby.

'I can't think of anything better,' he admitted.

'Don't forget, there's a guard on the cabin now.'

Toby smiled. 'The guard hasn't been born that I can't get past ... but tomorrow. We all need a night's sleep first.'

Outside, he told Ray, 'We'll be sleeping with Millie and Monty tonight. No sense in telling everyone where we are.'

* ★ ★ ★

Blackie leaned on the counter in the Silver Spur, one foot resting on the brass rail, contemplating a woman's navel. The woman was a reflection in the mirror behind the bar of a painting.

'Don't,' O'Brien warned.

Blackie removed his hand from the butt of his revolver. He gave a weak grin; it was a tempting target but Paddy was not a man to upset.

The saloon-owner looked to be a mild man of slight build compared to Blackie's size, but it didn't pay to upset him. A comment about O'Rourke's bald head by one of Carver's crew had found the speaker outside and unconscious almost before the words were out of his mouth.

Blackie had been in the saloon since

relaying Harknett's message to the marshal to run Small out of town. He'd stayed to see that, wondering what trick the stranger might pull. Disappointingly, he'd left when Lee ordered him out.

So Blackie felt cheated and headed for the bar and a drink and a moan to O'Rourke.

But the saloonman had said, 'That's fine with me. I'm not wanting trouble.'

It was starting to get dark and Blackie decided, finally, that he ought to ride back to the Crooked L. That was when Lee stepped through the batwings and came straight to the bar.

The marshal did not look happy.

'Blackie, when you get back, tell Mr Harknett that Miss Ella is good and mad and threatening reprisals.

'According to her, your foreman pushed her off the top of a canyon into the river — and she's going to print the story in her paper, calling it attempted murder.'

'Harknett won't like that,' Blackie

said, swallowing the last of his whiskey in a hurry.

'Neither will Carver,' O'Rourke said, 'and he's one I'd rather not tangle with.' He paused. 'Come to that, neither would I if it's likely to affect business with the dudes.'

'Figure most folk in town won't go for it either,' Lee said.

As the Crooked L man strode towards the door, the saloonman called:

'Hang on a minute, Blackie. I've got an idea.'

He turned to the marshal. 'Mr Lee, you won't want to hear this . . . and if there's a spot of bother at the paper's office tonight, don't go rushing there. Take your time.'

The lawman nodded and left.

O'Rourke said, 'Blackie, I reckon when yuh tell Harknett what she plans, he's going to say smash the press and she won't be able to print anything. Right?'

Blackie nodded. 'Sounds likely enough.'

'So save yourself another ride. Wait

till later and . . . '

'Makes sense,' Blackie said, and pushed his empty glass across the counter. 'Give me a refill, Paddy. I might as well wait here.'

He relaxed again. It would be best to wait till she was asleep; some folk got excited if you hurt a woman. The Silver Spur filled and emptied. It was dark when he went outside and got his horse and hitched it near the *Trumpet* office for a quick getaway; this job, he thought, was bound to make a bit of noise.

There was still a light showing in the office. After a time two figures came out; they looked like Small and the boy. But that wasn't possible, was it? Blackie blinked rapidly. Should he tell the marshal? The two figures didn't go into the hotel, so . . .

The hell with it. Stopping Miss Ella printing that story was more important. Lee would see Small in the morning.

He waited in a doorway. Lights went out one by one; sounds died away.

Main Street became deserted and silent. He waited a bit longer; let her get to sleep. He flexed his muscles, smiling.

Then he crossed the road and tried the door of the newspaper office. Locked. He leaned his weight against it; the latch gave way and the door swung open on to darkness. He left the door open and waited for his sight to adapt to the gloom inside.

He saw the shape of the press and, beyond it, wooden frames filled with type; paper was piled up all around.

He shoved over a few piles of paper first, tipped the racks of type on to them, and then a can of thick oily ink. He wrestled with the press; it was heavy but he was big and had muscles. He strained till it went over, smashing down on the jumbled type.

The noise echoed in the silence of the night and he thought, that's enough. He chuckled as he ran for his horse. She wouldn't be using that machine in a hurry.

He swung into the saddle as a figure

in white showed in the doorway. A rifle blasted, almost knocking him out of the saddle. He used spurs and his mount went into a gallop, leaving town fast.

There was wetness running down his arm and his shoulder hurt like hell. The cow had shot him! The sooner he reached the ranch the better.

★ ★ ★

When the train stopped at Snake City, Robert Frederick moved in his unhurried way to the baggage compartment to collect his saddle and rifle. He wore a suit, with flat-heeled boots, a string tie, a Stetson with a big crown, and carried a carpet-bag.

At the depot office, he asked, 'Can I leave my gear here?'

The clerk decided not to argue; this passenger had the lean and hungry look of a wolf.

'Yes, sir. Your name, sir?'

Robert Frederick told him and the man wrote out a receipt.

'Staying long, sir?'

'A few days, I expect.'

The clerk gave a knowing nod.

'Enjoy the hanging, sir.'

Frederick walked outside and on along the plankwalk with easy strides. He noted people and buildings and passed the hotel with only a glance. He continued till he came to Isaac's Boarding and Lodging House and went inside.

'Can I have a room at the front?'

Isaac was well-fed with a fleshy nose and sideburns. He held out his hand.

'For a dollar in advance, yes.'

Frederick paid him and carried his bag upstairs. The room was small but reasonably clean. He washed in cold water and put on a clean shirt. He left his gunbelt at the bottom of the bag, under riding-boots and a change of socks.

He stood by the window, looking out; opposite, across the width of Main Street, he saw a bank.

A voice called from below, 'Dinner's up.'

He went down and found the dining-room. There seemed to be only one other resident: a young man with blond hair and a cheeky expression.

'This young man is Silas.' Isaac introduced them. 'A regular here — he works as a clerk for Mr Chancellor, at the bank just across the way.'

Frederick nodded casually.

12

The Golden Lure

When Toby set out in the morning, Ella was looking serious and carried her rifle. Ray was excited at the prospect of returning to the cabin in the box canyon to free Mr Wallace.

They rode together on the wagon, with three horses on a lead behind: Ella's grey and two hired mounts. When he came to the trail leading off to the hills, Toby reined in his mules.

Ella and Ray climbed down and untied the horses. They had one each, and Ella led the spare for Wallace, assuming they were successful.

Toby said, 'Don't try rushing in. Wait out of sight till I persuade the guard to leave. This will take some time because I have to prepare the ground — but it'll work, you can be sure of that.'

He turned the wagon and urged Millie and Monty forward, following the trail that led into the wood near the river. He left the wagon among the trees and went forward on foot, carrying a canvas sack.

He reached the river and edged carefully along the wet rock path till he got close to the rapids. He took his time looking for the right spot — his trap had to be convincing.

He looked for cracks in the rock face and wedged the dust from his canvas sack into these. The dust was a dull yellow colour but, when sunlight struck it, the dust sparkled and caught his eye. Looks good, he decided, and returned to the wagon and urged Millie and Monty into motion.

He crossed the prairie and entered the box canyon without seeing any sign of Crooked L men or Ella and Ray. As he neared the cabin, he slowed his approach.

The man on guard covered him with a rifle and said, 'Freeze!'

Toby reined back, smiling. 'A strange way to greet the man who's going to make you wealthy.'

'I hope,' grunted the swarthy-faced guard.

'Your wish is granted.' Toby brought a small pouch from his pocket and tossed it to Carver's man.

Guzman caught it one-handed and opened it; he tipped yellow dust out and scattered it.

'Fool's gold,' he said contemptuously.

Toby sighed and shook his head. 'It's the real thing, but don't worry — there's plenty more where that came from.'

'And where's that?' Guzman was fingering some of the dust again, more carefully this time. 'What's the deal?'

'Not far from here. The point is, it's difficult for me to get at on my own. With two men, that's a different thing, that's why I'm looking for a partner. One who can keep his mouth buttoned.'

Guzman was almost convinced; as he

should be, for the small pouch contained the genuine stuff.

Toby looked at the gun covering him.

'You'll not find the vein without me. I reckon you can be there and back in a couple of hours. The two of us can clean up.'

He watched the guard's eyes and, when he saw greed there, he knew he'd won.

'Yes or no? I can easily find someone else to help me.'

'Yeah,' Guzman finally decided. 'I'll go along, but no tricks mind.'

'No tricks,' Toby agreed smoothly. 'Trust me!'

Guzman patted his rifle. 'This says how far I trust yuh.' As he climbed aboard the wagon, Toby turned the mules and started back.

It was a silent ride. Guzman watched Toby, and he carefully avoided looking for Ella and Ray, hidden somewhere nearby. He left the box canyon and drove down the slope towards the woods and the river beyond.

He pulled Millie and Monty to a halt among the trees.

'Now we walk. It's not far, just difficult to reach.'

Beside the swift-flowing river, Toby moved confidently along the narrow track with Guzman following, still carrying his rifle. Closer to the falls, Toby watched where he put his feet; the rock path was slippery with spray, and the noise of the falls echoed between canyon walls and turned to a thunderous roar.

'Somewhere here,' Toby shouted. 'Can you see anything yet?'

He half turned his head to look back. Guzman's eyes shone with greed; he was hooked. Then sunlight pierced the spray and struck the rock wall.

The fool's gold Toby had planted earlier glittered like a party bauble and Guzman shouted, 'There!'

He reached for the bright glints in the cracks as he brought his gun up. Toby sprawled flat on the path.

The rifle fired and the recoil pushed

Guzman off balance. His boots skidded on the treacherous surface and he lurched sideways, arms cartwheeling, feet gripping air. He lost his rifle and Toby made a grab for it.

Guzman fell, hit the river and went under, mouth open and swallowing water. The current snatched him and smashed him against one rock after another, dragging him to the brink of the falls. His greed had gone, replaced by fear.

Now he was desperate for help, but his screams were choked off as he went over the edge of the rapids and vanished from sight.

No chance, Toby thought.

★   ★   ★

Ray, with Ella, came out of hiding after Toby's wagon passed by. They rode quietly, Ella leading the spare horse, towards the cabin among the trees. There was no-one about.

'You go in first,' Ella said. 'He knows you.'

Ray dismounted and walked to the door, paused. He heard a low moaning from inside.

'He's hurt!'

He lifted the bar clear and dropped it. As he opened the door a weak voice said, 'No . . . no more, please . . . '

He went in quickly. 'It's me, Ray. I'm back with help. This time, we'll get you away.'

'Ray . . . ?'

Wallace seemed to be in a daze. He tried to sit up and fell back. 'No strength. My feet . . . '

Ray saw that his boots and socks had been removed; the soles of his feet were burnt black.

'Miss Ella — I can't manage on my own!'

Ella came in and saw the condition of his feet. 'Who did this?' she demanded.

'Carver . . . '

She raised her rifle.

'When I see Carver, he's dead meat, so don't concern yourself about him again.' She was still smarting over the wreckage of her press. Someone was going to pay . . .

'Ray, get yourself under his left arm. I'll take his right — now lift. Mr Wallace, keep your feet off the ground.'

Stumbling, they got the injured man outside to the spare horse.

'Grab the saddle horn, Mr Wallace, and haul up when we lift. Think you can stay in the saddle?'

Wallace made a weak smile.

'Guess I'll have to, ma'am.'

They set off, moving slowly. When they reached the mouth of the canyon, Toby's wagon was waiting.

Toby took one look and lifted Wallace from the saddle and laid him flat in the back of the wagon. He handed Guzman's rifle to Ella.

'Figure we might need more fire-power when Harknett finds his prisoner missing.'

'One down?' Ella asked, and Toby nodded.

'Good!'

Ray said, seriously, 'We'll fight better

on a full stomach. I'm starving!'

Toby took up the reins and headed for Tumbleweed.

★   ★   ★

Marshal Lee sat in his office polishing his badge. He whistled happily, pleased with life and himself. He wasn't often pleased with his performance; he was, he suspected, a weak character.

He'd failed at so many jobs he'd tried; as cook on a trail drive, the men had actually threatened to shoot him; as a school-teacher he'd found the boys were tougher than he was; he'd even tried farming till his back gave out.

But now he seemed to have found his niche. With Harknett and Carver backing him, he could hold his own as town marshal. The dudes were no bother. And hadn't Small left town when he'd told him to?

Life was improving. Anything might be possible in the future. A lawman was respected, looked up to . . .

He frowned as he glanced out of the door, hardly able to believe his eyes. A wagon looking very much like Small's came rumbling along Main Street. It *was* Small, as if he'd never been warned to quit town.

He pinned on his badge, picked up a shotgun and strode purposefully towards the wagon as it stopped outside the hotel.

'You!' he yelled. 'Yes, you, Small, I don't want you in town. I've told you that. You deaf or something?'

Toby ignored him. With Ella, he helped Wallace out of the wagon.

Lee stared, feeling sure this was one of the dudes from the Crooked L.

'What's going on? What have you done to this man?' he demanded. 'I've a good mind to arrest you on a charge of — '

'Marshal,' Wallace interrupted, 'it's not these good people you need to arrest. He, and Miss Ella and the boy rescued me. I've been held prisoner. It's Harknett and Carver you want.'

Lee, confused, mumbled, 'I can't believe that.'

'You'd better believe it,' Wallace said grimly. 'As soon as I get back East I shall be demanding that the federal law investigate here. You would do well to co-operate.'

'You can start now,' Ella added. 'I winged the man who wrecked my press — likely you'll find him at the Crooked L too.'

Between them, Toby and Ella helped Wallace into the hotel.

'I'm off to get the doctor,' Ella said.

'And I'm going to Cookie's to get something to eat,' Ray said.

Lee stared blankly, his world crumbling. He felt nervous and uncertain.

If Harknett and Carver were outside the law when they appointed him, and a federal marshal arrived . . . surely not even Miss Ella could expect him to go up against Carver?

He unpinned his badge and dropped it in the dust. 'I just resigned, so leave me out of it.'

From the doorway of the Silver Spur, Van and O'Rourke watched him walk away. The half-breed felt only contempt.

O'Rourke murmured, 'I hate a quitter. Guess Carver will be interested.'

Van nodded and went for his horse.

★　★　★

Frederick stood outside Isaac's lodging house watching the folk of Snake City go by. He appeared in no hurry to go about his own business, and seemed to merely glance at his surroundings.

In fact, his eyes were keenly noting every point of interest and assessing distances. He made mental notes of hitching rails, alleyways, the sheriff's office, Jackson's store and the Longhorn.

A sharp voice interrupted his thoughts.

'Are you here to see the hanging?'

It was young Silas, from the bank.

Frederick gave him a quiet smile.

'No, I've seen my share of that. It doesn't interest me now.'

'Yeah, you look like a man who's been around. Not always on the side of the law, perhaps?'

'I've been in places where the law can hardly be said to exist.'

'Perhaps we should worry with you standing there, sizing up our bank?'

Frederick nodded. 'Perhaps you should . . . On the other hand, you've reminded me of my purpose here. I came into some money and decided to invest it out West — mining, land, ranching, property — anything where the value is likely to go up.'

Silas smirked. 'You're not just moving money from one bank to another, are you?'

'Would it worry yuh?'

'No, sir. You've come to the right place — Snake City is going to boom.'

'I'm glad to hear that.'

'Mr Chancellor, who owns the bank, has an interest in several properties round about. You'll find him a keen adviser where there's a profit to be made. Shall I make an appointment for you to see him?'

Frederick considered this. 'Yeah, why not? I can use some professional advice.'

Silas said briskly, 'Good. I'll fix it, and let you know when this evening.'

13

Snake's Eyes

Carver glared at Blackie and snorted. 'A man your age should know better than to turn his back on anyone, especially a woman. Anyway, it wasn't Miss Ella — she's at the bottom of the rapids. I wonder who it was at her place?'

Harknett said, 'Maybe we ought to find out.'

'It was Miss Ella,' Blackie insisted. 'You can ask Mr Lee.' He turned to appeal to the Crooked L rancher. 'How about paying a bit more now there's lead flying?'

Carver nodded, irritated, 'It's only a flesh wound, that's nothing.'

'It's my flesh, and it hurts.'

Harknett poured himself a whiskey. 'You'll be paid when Wallace pays up.'

'And that'll be soon,' the foreman said grimly. 'I'm losing patience with that one.'

From the veranda, he looked across the range, hat pulled down to shield his eyes. A rider was coming fast towards the house. He scowled. 'It's Van — what's gone wrong now?'

The half-breed reined his horse and slid from the saddle. Ignoring Harknett, he spoke directly to Carver.

'Toby Small and the boy, just got into town with Miss Ella. They had Wallace with them — and the dude told Lee he was going to bring in federal law.' Van spat. 'That useless Lee took off his badge pronto.'

Carver stood motionless, thinking furiously. His first reaction was disbelief. How could anyone survive those rapids? And get Wallace away? But if Blackie was right, anything was possible.

Grudgingly, he called to Yuma, who was squatting on a corral fence, smoking. 'Get out to the cabin and check what's happened to Guzman.'

Yuma roped a horse, saddled it and rode away.

Harknett had lost colour. 'I don't understand how this has happened. What do we do now?'

'Wait till we know for sure. I'm still not convinced.'

The rancher reached for his Southern Comfort bottle. 'This is your fault, Carver. When Wallace gets to Snake City, the boss will . . . '

Carver stared at him with his unwinking eyes, and touched the butt of his revolver.

'Just keep the dudes off my back, that's all you have to do. I'll take care of the rest.'

'One of them — Mr Ambrose — has already gone into town. He's sweet on Miss Ella.'

The foreman barked out a laugh.

'Too bad for him! Too bad for anyone who gets in my way now. Since the boss has gone back, I'm taking charge and, if necessary, I'll kill them all. I'm going to rest. Let me know when Yuma gets back.'

Carver strode away to his room, the one with thick curtains permanently across the window. He closed the door, despite the heat, and lay on his bed with a dark cloth across his eyes, remembering . . .

In his early days, when he was still young enough to ignore warnings from experienced hunters, he'd ridden ahead of their party on his own.

He came to a grove of trees beside a river and saw a squaw, her back to him, walking away. She was apparently unaware of him, and his blood was up. She was just too easy to resist and he rushed forward.

The braves of her tribe had been waiting in ambush. A thrown axe stunned him.

When he recovered consciousness, he found himself staked to the ground on his back and staring at a cloudless sky. There was no shade and the sun blazed down on him.

He tried to shut his eyes against the glare and found they'd left his scalp but removed his eyelids. He couldn't blot out that burning horror in the sky. The squaw laughed and spat at him.

'White dog never look on squaw again!'

They went away, leaving him to stare endlessly at a golden yellow ball that filled his whole world without interruption. He'd never dreamed such torment possible.

He struggled to free himself and failed; he couldn't move sufficiently even to turn his head away from that terrible burning heat.

The position of the sun told him it was still morning; he had all day to suffer before darkness came. Except that it could only be a short time before he went blind.

He cursed and raved till his parched throat stopped him, staring at the sun and unable to close his eyes to bring relief. Sunlight flooded down from a blue sky, relentless; his merciless enemy.

Dazzling heat seared his eyeballs.

He could only stare upwards and curse inwardly and make useless promises of revenge. The awful fear of permanent blindness crept upon him. He would have cried if the sun had not evaporated the moisture.

It was the only time in his life he'd been truly afraid; after that experience, nothing could scare him.

It was the only time he'd screamed for help; never again he promised himself. He'd screamed — though it came out a croak — when he felt his sight going.

Consciousness gave way to madness.

Someone found him before it was too late. He recovered his sight, though he rested in the dark for two weeks before venturing outside in daylight. It was the last time he was grateful to another human being.

The end of fear left an enduring hatred. He would never be captured again; he would kill first.

He practised drawing his revolver and

shooting every day till he was both fast and accurate. He could clear holster and pull the trigger in one smooth movement — and hit his target even when it was moving. He built a reputation that other men were reluctant to challenge. He survived by killing and learned to despise weakness in everyone else; in Harknett, in Blackie, in Lee . . .

He lived in a darkened room behind a curtain. He slept with a cloth covering his eyes and his dreams were violent.

★　★　★

He woke with a start, sweating, staring unblinking because he had no eyelids to blink with. He put his hat on and pulled the brim low when he heard Yuma arrive back.

On the veranda, he kept in shadow.

Yuma said, 'There's no sign of Guzman, though his horse is still there. Wallace has gone.'

Carver nodded curtly. It always

seemed to come down to him to get other people out of trouble. Most men were simply not ruthless enough.

'All right.' He turned towards Harknett. 'We'll need extra guns and ammo — I'm taking every man I've got.'

'And I have a ranch to run,' Harknett protested. 'Eastern dudes to look after.'

'Wallace has got to be stopped before he opens his mouth. Everyone he talks to must be killed.' Carver's expression was savage. 'I'm concerned with looking after me — and unless we stop this dude, you won't have a ranch at all.'

The half-breed, Van, had been listening with more than casual interest. He drawled, 'Mr Harknett, how much to kill Wallace?'

Harknett thought about it. Van was not directly employed by the Crooked L — he was Carver's man. This might be a way out.

'A hundred bucks, cash in hand. Without Wallace, there's no proof against us.'

Van grinned broadly. 'Half now, cash.'

The rancher went into the house and returned with a handful of notes. He counted out fifty dollars.

Van climbed into the saddle. 'Relax, man. Wallace is dead!'

★　★　★

Judge Benson in a flannel nightgown was not the intimidating sight he appeared in black robes.

In the early hours, he was awake and unhappy. His face was bleached of its usual ruddy colour and his gaunt frame appeared skeletal.

His day in Redstone had gone well; one trial after another, bullying the jury into condemning yet another villain and handing out a few years' hard labour. A successful day, but involving only small-time criminals.

It was the evening that had ruined things. The mayor and the sheriff had insisted on a celebration dinner at the local hotel. The main course had been reasonable, though he'd eaten too much of it; the pudding had been heavy as lead shot, the liqueurs sickly and his cigar of the green variety. The dinner had lasted a couple of hours and how he regretted every minute of it.

He lay in bed, alone, groaning. His stomach felt as if it contained a jagged lump of the famous red sandstone that gave the town its name. Or perhaps cooling lava from a volcano. He alternately sweated and shivered and his temper was foul. If he had one of those small-time crooks handy at that moment, it would have been a hanging job.

He stared at the grey gloom beyond the window pane and prayed for dawn. As soon as it was light, he would travel. He shifted his position again and moaned as fresh pain started up.

It was no good; he had to lie flat on his back to get any relief at all. The smoke-blackened ceiling was not inspiring. The building was remarkably quiet;

must be sometime in the early hours, he thought. How much longer to dawn? The pain seemed to increase and he moaned and groaned but nobody heard, nobody cared.

This was dreadful. He promised himself that as soon as he reached Snake City, there'd be no delay. None. A quick trial, a guilty verdict and an immediate hanging. That was the only cure for an upset stomach.

14

Two Dudes

Ambrose didn't feel relaxed in the saddle, although he was beginning to get used to the Western model. Back in Boston, a riding-saddle was quite a bit different. His face burned where it had caught the sun, and his new clothes still felt stiff.

But he liked the fresh air and sense of freedom after the restrictions of Eastern society. He liked the idea of living close to nature, and he was a little bit in love with Miss Ella.

He had a vague dream that he would one day buy a ranch, and was still dreaming when he reached Tumbleweed and rode along Main Street to her studio. He had some prints to collect, but they were really only an excuse to see her again.

He dismounted and tied his horse to a hitching rail and pushed open the door. He was surprised to find her on hands and knees sorting type that had been spilled on the floor. The press was on its side and everywhere there were piles of scattered paper smeared with ink.

'What on earth . . . ? Has there been an accident?'

Ella came to her feet, unsmiling. 'No accident. Have you got a Crooked L man back there with a gunshot wound?'

'Why, yes, how did you know? Blackie had an accident with — '

'Blackie, was it? Waal, I was that accident, and next time I see him I'll finish the job!'

As Ambrose struggled to help her get the heavy press upright, he appreciated the way feminine muscles filled her jeans and shirt. He asked, 'Why would Blackie do this?'

'Because he had orders to stop the story I intend to print,' she said with a touch of bitterness. 'Orders from

Harknett — or, more likely, Carver. It's time you dudes woke up to what's going on.'

'What's that?'

'I was thrown off a cliff to drown in the rapids — along with young Ray — by Carver and his bunch. If it hadn't been for Toby Small neither of us would be here to testify against the Crooked L.'

He stared blankly at her. 'You're serious?'

'I'm serious. And you should see what they did to one of your own. Dude named Wallace — '

'Wallace? He's back?'

'I don't know about back. Maybe he was never away? He's at the hotel. The doc says he'll recover eventually, but he won't be walking for a while.'

'This is alarming. I thought he'd returned home . . . '

'Maybe you'd better talk to him yourself.'

'Yes, I certainly will.'

Ambrose left the studio and walked

across Main Street to the hotel. Ella
snatched up her rifle and followed him,
aware that she was watched by the
people of Tumbleweed, who could see
their livelihood threatened.

Wallace had a room on the ground
floor. She knocked and called:

'It's me, Ella.'

The door was unlocked by Toby. Ray
sat beside a couch, holding a rifle.

Ambrose, astonished, said, 'It is you,
Wallace. We all thought you'd gone
back East.'

'That was my intention. Excuse me
not getting up, Ambrose. You can see
why . . . ' Wallace, lying full length on
the couch, raised a blanket to show his
bare feet.

Ambrose started. 'Good God! How —?'

'Not how,' Wallace said bleakly. 'Who.
And the answer is Carver — because I
wouldn't sign his bit of paper.'

Toby moved a chair up and Ambrose
sat down. 'What the devil's been going
on?'

Wallace smiled weakly. 'As you know,

I was returning after my vacation. Carver was to drive me into Snake City to meet the train.

'Well, we didn't get there, and I ended up in a hidden canyon where I was shut in a cabin and held prisoner. The idea, of course, was to collect ransom money — but they miscalculated. I have no close relatives in a position to pay what they demanded. Carver tried to force me to sign a paper ordering my bank to send money to Snake City. Naturally, I refused.'

Ambrose looked bewildered, and Wallace added:

'Apparently, I'm not the first. But they had no difficulty collecting before.'

'They? Do you mean . . . ?'

'Oh, yes, Harknett's in it up to his neck. And someone else, who hides behind a mask. But it's that foreman who scares me . . . '

Ella said, irritated, 'I've told you, forget Carver. The moment I get him in my sights, he's dead.'

'The whole crew at the ranch is in it.

Sure, it's run as a vacation ranch — but a few selected victims are hidden away and money demanded for their return.'

Ambrose still seemed doubtful. 'And Marshal Lee?'

'He was Harknett's appointment,' Ella said. 'He may not have known. All he had to do was obey orders. I don't suppose many in town knew. The ranch was good for business and we shut our eyes. I know I did.'

Ambrose said slowly, 'I suppose I have to believe now — even in a mystery man!'

'He's the one who gives the orders. But Carver, his staring eyes . . . ' Wallace shivered. 'He actually boasted to me he'd killed a United States Marshal, shot him in the back — '

Toby suddenly came to life. '*What?* Are you sure?'

'That's what he said. Apparently this was in Snake City one evening.'

Toby said, excited, 'I want to get you to Snake City quickly, Mr Wallace. Are you up to the journey?'

'I'll stand anything that puts distance between me and that cold-blooded devil!'

'Good. Ray, hitch the mules ready to go and bring the wagon round to the hotel. Mr Wallace, my brother's been accused of that murder. I need you to repeat your story to the sheriff.'

'I want to see the sheriff myself!'

'I'll come with you,' Ambrose said.

'And me,' Ella said. 'Mr Ambrose, I suggest a rifle and as much ammunition as you can afford.'

Toby went to Mac's with Ambrose to stock up for the journey. He wondered, briefly, why Carver had ambushed a marshal; not that it mattered. The dude's story would save George.

Between them, they carried Wallace out to the wagon. Ella hurried from her studio with a small leather bag. Toby climbed into the driving-seat and Ray sat with Wallace in the back.

They set off from Tumbleweed, with Ambrose and Ella on horseback, watched by the townsfolk.

* * *

Van rode quietly into town, unhurried and relaxed. He was feeling good, fifty bucks in his pocket and a white man relying on him. As a half-breed he got his share of insults, and not only from white men: some Indians could show that they, too, despised a 'breed.

He assumed Wallace would be staying at the hotel, but he'd had one unfortunate experience there, so he hitched his horse behind the Silver Spur and used the back way in. He walked straight to the bar and ordered whiskey.

O'Rourke looked sharply at him as he poured.

'What did Carver say?'

Van gave a half smile. 'Carver can be a bit slow sometimes — I spoke to Harknett. Is Wallace still at the hotel?'

'You missed 'em. The doc patched up Wallace and there's ugly rumours circulating about the Crooked L. Wallace is travelling aboard Small's wagon, with the kid, aiming to see the sheriff at Snake City. Another dude, and Miss Ella, are riding shotgun.' O'Rourke paused. 'Doesn't sound good for business.'

The half-breed called for another drink while he considered the information.

Hell, a wagon — he'd soon catch up with that. But other people along could complicate matters. Luckily there were ways only an Indian knew . . .

'Don't quit yet,' he told the saloon owner. 'A lot of things can happen before Wallace reaches Snake City. And rumours last only till the next one comes along.'

'That's a fact.'

Van finished his drink at leisure. 'I'm going for a meal. I suppose Carver, or maybe Harknett, will be in sometime. Tell him I'm chasing Small's wagon, and that Wallace is aboard.'

He set down his glass and headed for the door. O'Rourke's nose wrinkled. He was used to all sorts, but Van's bear-grease turned his stomach.

★ ★ ★

Carver was riding for Tumbleweed, and not alone. He remembered that Van had failed once before, when he'd gone after Small. He couldn't afford to wait if the half-breed failed again. He had to make sure of Wallace; that one knew too much.

He kept his horse at an easy lope, along with Harknett and the whole crew of the Crooked L. And the dudes. The Easterners were excited, laughing and joking. It was a simple idea: they were to imagine they were cowboys at the end of a trail drive and riding to 'tree' the town.

Of course, they'd only be shooting into the air but, under cover of the excitement, Carver reckoned it would be easy enough to slip into the hotel and make sure of Wallace.

When he could see the town just ahead, he dug in his spurs and gave a wild yell.

'Shoot 'em up, boys!'

His crew, and the dudes, urged their mounts to a gallop, gripping revolvers. Hoofbeats thundered as they entered Main Street and raced along its length, shouting and shooting wildly at the false fronts above stores and saloons.

They charged to the far end then swung back again. Glass shattered; someone dived behind a water-barrel; a dog bolted for safety. It was a thrilling ride and nobody got hurt but, for a few minutes, startled faces peered from windows and blood ran hot and pulses pounded.

The riders finally came to a halt outside the Silver Spur, holstering empty guns. The dudes swaggered inside, feeling real tough *hombres*.

'Drinks on me, boys,' Harknett shouted, winking at the balding saloon owner. He noted that one of the crew — Carver — was missing.

The Easterners started card games, calling loudly for whiskey and beer, wine and brandy. Harknett put on his best Southern drawl to accommodate them.

Carver turned his mount into an alley that came out behind the hotel. He swung out of his saddle and looped the reins around a post. He opened a rear door and moved quietly along a passage.

He found nobody at the reception desk, nor in the dining-room. The whole building was suspiciously silent. He retreated to the kitchen where he found the hotel man pouring a slug of whiskey into a mug of coffee.

'What was the ruckus all about?'

'Just a bit of fun for the dudes,' Carver drawled. 'Nothing to get upset about. Seen Van lately?'

'Not today.'

Carver bit down on a curse. 'Which room is Wallace in?'

The hotel man gave a sly smile. 'He was here for a while. He's gone now.'

Carver froze. 'Gone? Where? How?'

'After Doc patched him up, he took a trip on Small's wagon heading for

Snake City. You ain't goin' to be so popular when . . . '

Carver fought to stay calm. He had to think. Forget the dudes — collect Harknett and the crew and get after that wagon . . .

'Where can I find Lee?'

'He does his drinking at Nick's place these days.'

'I heard he chucked his badge on the ground outside here.'

'Sure did, I — '

Carver held out his hand. 'Give.'

The hotel man hesitated. 'It must be worth — '

Carver whipped his gun out, level with the man's stomach; with his other hand he pulled a dollar bill from his pocket.

'One dollar — or a lead slug. Your choice.'

The hotel man hastily produced the marshal's silver badge and grabbed the dollar.

'Wise man.' Carver slipped the badge in his pocket, holstered his Colt and left. He walked across to the Silver Spur and spoke quietly to one of his crew. 'Round up all the boys, including Harknett. Ditch the dudes — we're riding.'

He moved on to Nick's place, an old-style saloon that hadn't been renovated; a few diehards used it, preferring to avoid the Easterners. He found Lee at a corner table with a bottle and glass; one of the saloon girls was helping him drown his sorrows. Carver tapped her on the shoulder.

'Find another mug, sister. I want this one.'

She gave him a startled look, snatched up her glass and left hurriedly.

A silence descended on Nick's place. It seemed most customers had stopped breathing; eyes swivelled to take in the table where the ex-marshal sat alone. Bets were laid and someone murmured, 'Just call the undertaker.'

Lee's face was pale and beads of sweat gathered on his forehead; he avoided the foreman's staring eyes and watched his gun hand, knowing he hadn't a chance. His lips were dry.

'If you figure you can beat me, draw,' Carver said, and his revolver was suddenly in his hand pointing at Lee's face, finger around the trigger.

Seconds like years passed and Carver didn't fire.

Lee licked his lips. 'What d'yuh want?'

Carver pulled the badge from his pocket. 'Put that back on.'

Lee's nervous fingers fumbled, but he finally managed it.

'Outside, and get your horse. We're riding.'

Fresh air sobered the rc-appointed lawman. At the stable he saddled his bronc, keenly aware he was still alive.

'What's this all about?'

Carver waited till Harknett and the crew of the Crooked L gathered.

'All present will raise their right hand. Now deputize us, Marshal.'

Startled, Lee mumbled the words.

'Right,' Carver said. 'Wallace is

aboard Small's wagon and we're going to stop them reaching Snake City. You, Lee, will call on Small's party to surrender to the law. They won't, of course, so they'll die resisting arrest — all perfectly legal and we're in the clear. Let's ride.'

15

The Blooding

It was not long before Van saw dust rising from wagon wheels on the main trail ahead of him. He swerved across country to pick up a secondary trail running parallel; he wanted to get in front. If they anticipated an attack, it would be from behind.

He knew of a slight rise where cottonwoods could hide him from view, and pushed his horse till he arrived. There was no sign of the wagon, so he stripped the saddle from his horse and composed himself to wait.

He smiled a little. The despised half-breed would soon be collecting another fifty dollars from Harknett. He stripped down to a breech cloth and selected his weapon: another arrowhead. He liked to get to grips with an enemy.

He watched the wagon grow in size as it came closer, at a slightly lower level. Miss Ella and a dude were riding horses; Small was driving — that left only the kid inside with Wallace. His lip curled: easy meat.

He waited for the right moment, then swung up to ride bareback and sent his horse galloping down the slope . . .

★　★　★

It was a long haul to Snake City so, after getting well clear of Tumbleweed, Toby allowed Millie and Monty to set their own pace.

Ella, armed with a rifle, rode slightly in advance of the mules; Ambrose, similarly armed, followed behind. Wallace stretched out in the back of the wagon, under the canvas hood, with Ray who also held a rifle.

Toby had a single idea, to deliver Wallace to the sheriff so he could say his piece. Once George was freed, he could wash his hands of the whole business and get back to his own life.

The plain rolled on before him, seemingly endless; but somewhere the mules could smell water and quickened their pace. The trail dipped slightly as it passed a stand of cottonwoods.

Then Ella raised her rifle and snapped off a shot. Toby came alert, and Millie and Monty broke into a brisk trot; they'd heard gunfire before.

Toby saw a riderless horse come galloping down the slope from the trees and wondered why Ella had fired. The horse was suddenly racing alongside the wagon and he realized it wasn't riderless.

Its rider had been lying along the far side of the animal, Indian-style, out of sight. Now the rider swung up, weapon gripped between his teeth. He vaulted from his horse on to the side of the wagon. One slash at the canvas and he was inside.

Toby smelt bear-grease and cursed.

He turned, groping for his hidden Derringer, and shouted:

'Ray! Stop him!'

Ray saw the intruder push through the gap in the canvas and recognized the weapon as he lunged for Wallace lying on a blanket on the wood floor. It was a hand-held arrowhead. The face above it might have been mistaken for an Indian.

Wallace gasped and tried to roll away.

Ray's rifle came up in a reflex action, the muzzle almost touching the half-breed; his finger jerked the trigger.

There was a muffled explosion and the attacker shuddered, grunted, and collapsed, bleeding from a chest wound. His hand still gripped his weapon.

Ray suddenly realized he'd killed a man and felt sick. His face lost colour.

Wallace pushed the body away from him.

'That was the right thing to do, Ray. You saved my life.'

Toby slowed the wagon. Ella came alongside and climbed on. She untied the canvas at the back and pushed the body out.

Ambrose's horse, coming up behind, shied as the corpse hit the ground in front of it. The dude recognized Van and lost his last doubt about his friend's story.

Ella got the boy's head outside as he vomited. Then she hugged him: he was shivering.

'It's all right, Ray. He was going to kill Mr. Wallace. You *had* to shoot. You'll get over it.'

She called to Toby: 'Keep going — the others may be on their way!'

★ ★ ★

Polly Small was worried about more than George. She felt heavy, sick and lonely. Sometimes she wondered how much longer she could go on.

George, of course, was still moaning about his brother. 'Why doesn't he get me out of here? Where is he? What is he doing?'

When she left the cell with an empty dish, she felt near collapse and sat down in the nearest chair.

Sheriff Nash viewed her with alarm.

'Are you . . . ? I'll get my wife,' he said, and rushed out in a panic. Now was no time to tell her the judge had reached his last stop before Snake City; and the word was he was in a hurry to get here.

Polly stared blindly in front of her, eyes filling with tears. This should be the happiest time of her life. They'd both wanted to start a family, but now . . .

Anna Nash walked in, took one look and put her arms around her.

'Such righteous women, your church people. Come with me, my dear — I'll make you soup the German way. And *schnitzel*. You must keep up your strength.'

Polly struggled upright and Anna helped her to the door.

Nash began to protest.

'Not our home, please. Remember I'm the sheriff and — '

Anna gave him a look. 'And Polly is a

180

woman who stands by her husband, as I would stand by you — so no nonsense, please.'

The sheriff frowned. 'Mr Chancellor has already complained about seeing you with her. It's coming up to election time, and he's an important man in Snake City.'

'Important man,' Anna said with contempt. 'Polly is carrying a child and needs help. A banker only carries money.'

She helped Polly next door and sat her down, then bustled into the kitchen.

'Cheer up, my dear. Everything will be splendid. You'll have a fine baby, and let's hope it's a girl — boys, unfortunately, grow into men with stupid ideas.'

She returned with a hot dish which she set before Polly.

'Now, eat up.' She frowned. 'That ridiculous banker — the man's a fool!'

⋆   ⋆   ⋆

Carver set a fast pace. His mood was savage, and he'd made up his mind. It wasn't just Wallace and that interfering Small who would die; he'd wipe them all out.

That woman, Ambrose, the boy too. He would leave no-one alive to tell what really happened. As he rode his brain was active, planning ahead to throw suspicion elsewhere.

Harkness rode to one side, Lee on the other. Blackie, Lefty, Slim and Yuma were right behind.

The trail was clear to read and a wagon couldn't hide; it was only a question of time. As they passed some cottonwoods, Harknett pointed.

'There — looks like a body!'

Carver spared a glance. 'Yeah, Van — this time he's paid for failing.'

'We can't be far behind,' Lee said, anxiety in his voice.

He's got cold feet, Carver thought; and the sight of Van sprawled bloodily on the ground gave him an idea. He reined back and dismounted. The half-breed still clutched an arrowhead.

Carver forced it from his hand and

shoved it in his belt. He tore away the breech clout and a handful of dollars fluttered out; he gave a rough count, about thirty left. He got back in the saddle, grinning as he joined the others.

'Hold your hand out, Marshal.'

Lee obeyed, and Carver shoved the money into his hand.

'Now you're paid. Rat on me a second time and I'll put lead in your belly and force a canteen of water down your throat!'

The trail curved away to follow a bend in the river.

'This way,' Carver shouted, heading off the trail. 'We'll take a short cut and get ahead of them.'

They raced on till they came to a place where the trail swung back again, dipping between rocks.

'Here,' Carver said, dismounting. 'We'll wait in ambush — it won't be long now.'

His unwinking eyes studied the Crooked L crew.

'What we'll do is shoot the animals,

loot and burn the wagon. I've got one of Van's arrowheads, and we'll make it look like an Indian attack — then no-one will even look our way.' He laughed. 'I've always wanted to take a scalp, and now I will!'

Harknett's face was pale. 'You're talking massacre. If anyone suspected — '

'Stop bellyaching. Sometimes I think you've got a yellow streak. This is for real — Wallace has to die, and everyone with him!' Carver paused. 'Lee is our safety net. The marshal's in charge — we're his deputies, obeying orders.'

'Do we wear masks?' Yuma asked.

'There's no need. We're not leaving anyone alive to identify us . . . keep under cover now!'

He could hear wagon wheels and glimpsed the mules, with Miss Ella in the lead. His gun came up, drawing a bead on her.

★　★　★

Silas winked as he showed Robert Frederick into his boss's office in the Snake City bank.

'Mr Frederick, sir.'

Chancellor nodded.

'Take a seat, Mr Frederick.' He waited for Silas to withdraw. 'My clerk tells me you have money to invest.'

'That's right.' Frederick sat in a hard chair before Chancellor's desk; Chancellor's own comfortably padded armchair was raised on a platform. He liked to look down on those he intended to refuse giving a loan to.

Chancellor narrowed his eyes, staring intently at his visitor.

'Can I assume you came into this money legally?'

Robert Frederick nodded.

'Not that it matters as far as I'm concerned . . . but sometimes it's necessary to be careful.'

Frederick made a small smile. 'I see that I did right in seeking professional advice.'

'And now you wish to buy property?

Anything in mind? A ranch, for instance?'

Frederick shook his head. 'Property here in town, I guess. More likely to increase in value.'

The banker nodded approvingly. 'I see you have a head for business. Yes, I can offer several choices . . . you are aware that we have a hanging scheduled?'

'It would be difficult to avoid knowing.'

'I'm a law and order man myself,' Chancellor said, 'that goes without saying.'

'Me too,' Frederick said quickly. 'When a lawman is killed — as I believe is the case here — his killer must pay. You'll get no argument from me on that score.'

Chancellor nodded slowly, as if satisfied.

'Quite so. Well, I have mortgages on several choice businesses . . . '

Frederick nodded again, unsmiling. He was busy summing up his impressions of the banker: greedy, unscrupulous, ruthless and, most decidedly, not a fool.

* * *

Harknett felt despair. Not Ella, he thought, and found his voice. 'Ella, look out!' he shouted.

Carver fired, but her grey was already wheeling around and the shot went wild. Furiously, he turned on the Crooked L rancher.

'Stupid!' he screamed, and fired point blank.

Harknett was knocked backwards from his horse and was dead before he hit the ground.

Toby urged the mules to speed and the wagon with Ambrose aboard careered past. Random shots came Carver's way, but he ducked.

He swore violently, but it was too late to recover their advantage. The wagon was past and moving away.

'All right,' he said. 'We'll do it the hard way — they can't escape. We'll follow and pick them off, one by one.'

The Crooked L bunch spurred their horses in pursuit, guns blazing.

16

Brighter than Noon

Millie and Monty needed no urging. Their hoofs clattered over the trail at reckless speed; behind them the wagon swayed from side to side on creaking wheels while Toby searched anxiously for any cover where they might make a stand.

Ella dropped back to add her rifle to that of Ambrose at the rear as Crooked L riders galloped up, throwing slugs at them. In a long chase, Carver's superior force would wear them down.

Toby glimpsed a building ahead; it was not much of one, the roof gone and the walls partly collapsed, but it would provide some shelter. A derelict farmhouse, he guessed, and urged his mules to a final effort. It was, at least, cover and there was a chance they could hold out. They had no chance on the open prairie.

He drove headlong into the ruin and the mules stopped when they came to a standing wall. The wagon lurched to a standstill, swaying violently.

Ella and Ambrose galloped in, almost crashing into the mules and, for a moment, there was chaos. Ray unhitched Millie and Monty and they promptly lay down; they'd seen it all before. The two horses had to be persuaded to kneel.

Ray and Ella lifted Wallace from the wagon and hid him behind a wall.

'We'll fort up here,' Toby said. 'Be sparing with your ammo — make every shot count.'

'Carver's mine,' Ella snapped.

The chase caught up as Carver's outfit arrived, firing their revolvers.

'Just keep your heads down,' Toby murmured. 'The more ammunition they waste the better.'

A voice rang out.

'This is Marshal Lee. You are surrounded by my lawful posse — surrender now and you will receive a fair trial.'

Ella snorted and sent a shot winging that lifted Lee's hat.

Immediately guns sprayed the farmhouse with bullets, doing little damage. Now and again, Ella would pop up and send lead Carver's way, but he kept moving. The Crooked L men lacked cover and only their weaving mounts saved them.

Carver was anxious to reach Wallace, the one man who could put a noose around his neck; but eventually he caught on he wasn't getting anywhere.

'Back off,' he ordered. 'They're not going anyplace — we'll wait and rush them after dark.'

His riders split up, circling at a distance, watching from each point of the compass. They settled to wait for nightfall.

* * *

Frederick was strolling the boardwalk on Snake City's Main street, eyeing some of the property. He gave the appearance of taking it easy, not obviously studying the people.

Yet when a plump woman, her face flushed, shot out of Jackson's General Store like a bullet from a gun, Frederick lengthened his stride.

He saw Jackson follow her, apparently trying to change her mind.

The woman, obviously pregnant, said, 'I think that's terrible — you on the jury. You should be helping George!'

Jackson said desperately, 'Polly, I just wasn't thinking — of course I support George — even though I can't see he's got any chance. I'll resign from the jury . . .'

The woman hurried away, crying, 'He's innocent — George never shot anyone!'

As she left, Frederick arrived.

Jackson said, angrily, 'She's being unreasonable. Everyone knows her husband will hang. It's a sure thing — why shouldn't I start courting her?'

Frederick said gravely, 'Women are

often unreasonable, Mr Jackson — this is well known. Though perhaps you weren't thinking too clearly; a widow ain't likely to be partial to someone who helped hang her husband.'

The store-owner calmed down. 'Could be you're right, sir.' He saw Nash stepping along the boardwalk, and called, 'Sheriff!'

As Nash came up, he said, 'Sheriff, I'm withdrawing from jury service. Polly seems to have got the wrong idea . . . '

Nash nodded, and turned to study Frederick.

'Are you Robert Frederick?'

'That's me, Sheriff.'

'Mr Chancellor has suggested your name for jury service. A stranger in town, with no bias, so you can give a true verdict. What Mr Chancellor says is good enough for me. Are you willing to stand?'

Frederick smiled pleasantly. 'Sorry, but I'm not available.' He spoke in a relaxed drawl. 'I have other business here.'

They all three stared along the street as a shout came:

'Judge Benson's in town!'

★   ★   ★

Toby watched the daylight fade. From being a shelter, the old farmhouse could become a death-trap. When Carver attacked he'd know that, in the dark, everyone inside the walls was a target.

Toby looked about him and said quietly, 'Ray, hitch our mules and help Wallace into the back of the wagon. Then saddle the horses.'

Wallace tried to smile for the boy, but he was no hero. He'd learnt that these last few days. His mouth was dry and fear lay heavy on his heart; the fear that Carver would burn his feet again was like a nightmare. If he got out of this, he'd never leave Eastern society again. Out here, he felt useless, unable to cope with wild and reckless men. He would never fit in . . .

Toby said, 'We'll make a break for it and take our chances — we can't afford to let them rush us in the dark. That could be fatal.'

A crackle of gunfire indicated that Carver was getting impatient. Bullets slamming into clay walls gave them an incentive to hurry.

Ambrose fired back, warning the Crooked L men to keep their distance. He complained: 'It's getting harder to see them clearly.'

They prepared for the breakout, all except Ella; she, apparently, had her own programme. Rummaging among her gear, she brought out a small leather bag, and a metal tray mounted on a handle.'

'What have you got there?' Toby asked.

'If it works, a little surprise that could give us a big advantage.'

At last they were ready to make the break for freedom. Carver's men, on foot now, were edging closer.

'All ready?' Toby called softly. 'We'll

go in one rush, close together.'

'Two minutes,' Ella said. 'Just give me two minutes.'

* * *

Sheriff Owen Nash didn't like being rushed. He'd had George Small snug in jail all this time, waiting for the judge to arrive, so what was so urgent about his trial now? Tomorrow would do as well — or better.

'I don't like to waste time,' Benson said. 'The fellow's obviously guilty, so let's get on with it.'

Nash could see where the judge got his reputation. He'd hardly been in town long enough to wet his throat and still wore his Prince Albert coat and hat.

The sheriff chewed on a wad of tobacco.

'The mayor's not going to like it,' he warned. 'He wants a bit of pomp and ceremony — you know, declare a holiday, organize a street party. A lot of kids are keen and their parents don't want them staying up late to watch.'

He stroked his moustache. 'Besides, a good show is good for business.'

Benson wavered. Keen as he was, would another twelve hours make that much difference?

'Could be a slap-up do afterwards,' Nash tempted.

Gimlet eyes bored into him. 'I hope you're not trying to bribe me?'

'Of course not, Judge. Look at it this way. Snake City is growing and needs a more dignified style of hanging — not just the old hang 'em and forget 'em. We figure this way will act as a warning to any young 'un who might be tempted to go outside the law.'

Judge Benson hesitated, then nodded. 'It's true, the old ways are passing.'

He strode back to the cells and shouted between the bars: 'You've got one last night, Small, so practise saying your prayers. Tomorrow you'll hang higher than a kite!'

★ ★ ★

Ella untied the neck of the leather bag and carefully poured a white powder into the metal tray.

'Cover the animals' heads,' she warned. 'When I shout 'Now!' close your eyes, and don't open them till I tell you.'

She held up the metal holder, above a broken wall, and fumbled in her pocket for a match. She struck it.

'*Now!*'

She dropped the lighted match in the tray and closed her eyes, counting. The powder ignited.

To the Crooked L men, closing in on the farmhouse and watching intently for a target, the darkness blossomed with light brighter than noon. There was a brilliant white flare that dazzled; the powder burned with a blinding flame. They stared into it and could see nothing afterwards.

For Carver it was far worse than momentary blindness; it was the return

of his torment, the agony of sightless-
ness, and he screamed.

The flash lasted several seconds. Ella
raised her rifle, aimed by sound and put
a bullet in him.

Carver staggered, hit the ground and
rolled over, making choking noises.

The Crooked L men panicked.
Harknett was dead and now Carver was
down. They turned and ran for their
horses, Lee leading them. Blackie fired
back wildly, without coming near
hitting anybody.

'You can look now,' Ella said in a
voice that had the ring of satisfaction to
it.

Toby and Ambrose joined her at the
wall as hoofbeats receded in the
distance. Ray sent a couple of shots
after them, but it was wasted effort.

'Guess they won't be coming back,'
Toby said.

'What was that stuff?' Ambrose
asked.

'Magnesium powder. It was sold for
indoor photography so I got some to

try. It didn't work too well . . . but it sure is great for scaring off gunmen.'

She walked out to where Carver lay, followed by Toby.

It had not been a heart shot, and he still lingered. Tears oozed from lidless eyes and his pain was obvious when he tried to move. He seemed short of breath and blood frothed about his lips.

He appeared desperate to speak, even though he had difficulty. Ella thought it was a lung shot.

'I'm not going to make it, am I? I want you to know . . . it wasn't my idea to backshoot that marshal . . . I'd have faced him . . . the boss insisted, to avoid suspicion . . . it was an old gun I dropped beside him . . .'

He slumped back, exhausted.

'Who's this boss?' Ella demanded sharply.

Carver made a weak smile. 'No . . . you won't get that out of me.' He shuddered, and lay still.

Ella scowled. 'Carrion bait!'

'Waal, on to Snake City as soon as the moon rises,' Toby said.

17

Trial by Judge

George woke early with a sour taste in his mouth. Benson shouting through the bars last night had unsettled him; he felt sure that wasn't how a judge was supposed to behave. He'd been sleeping well before but this morning he was still half asleep.

He could hear hammering somewhere, and wondered what the time was. Did it matter? He rubbed a hand over the bristles on his jaw. Did anything matter any more? Was this really his last day on earth? A sense of panic threatened to overwhelm him, and he dropped to his knees and prayed.

The one thing in this situation that comforted him was that he hadn't lost his faith in the Lord.

The door of his cell opened and Nash came in with another man. George recognized him: Kemp, the mayor, who made his living as a blacksmith.

'Hold out your hands.'

George obeyed, and Kemp wrapped big hands around his wrists. After a few seconds he said, 'All right,' and left the cell.

George looked at the sheriff, mystified.

'Mr Kemp is going to make a pair of iron cuffs to fit, rather than use rawhide to tie your hands behind your back.'

The sheriff smoothed down his moustache. 'You're getting the royal treatment, Small. Carpenters are building a proper gallows right this minute.'

As the fat deputy came in with a pail of water, a bar of yellow soap and a rough towel, he added, 'And the mayor has declared today a public holiday, so you'd better wash up before you go on parade.'

'Can I have a razor?'

'Oh, no, I'm not risking that,' Nash

said quickly. 'Not at this stage of the proceedings.'

George had just finished washing when Polly arrived with his breakfast.

'Last time together,' the sheriff said, 'so I'll lock you in. You may attend the trial if you wish, Mrs Small, but I advise against trying to see the hanging. Anna will look after yuh, I'm sure.'

'There won't be a hanging,' Polly snapped back. 'George is innocent!'

'Depends how Benson decides, ma'am.'

The door closed, the key turned. Polly kissed her husband and hugged him for a long moment.

'Eat up, George. You'll need every bit of strength to stand up to Judge Benson.'

He ate slowly, his appetite fading with each mouthful.

'Will you be all right, Polly?' He fretted. 'I do wish Toby was here.'

'He'll be here,' Polly said loyally. 'And Mrs Nash has been kind.'

The cell door opened and Anna beckoned.

'Come with me, Polly. We'll slip in the back way.'

Nash fitted George's handcuffs.

'Let's go. It'll be the worse for you if we keep the judge waiting.'

There was a cheer from the crowd outside the jail as George was helped up on to a wagon. He stood straight, while one of the deputies drove to the courthouse.

George decided this was how an early Christian must have felt in Rome as he was led into the arena. The fat deputy waved to the crowd, who booed and jeered. Families with kids lined the route; they had come to town for a day's outing. Flags and bunting decorated Main Street . . . perhaps there would be fireworks tonight?

The sun shone in a cloudless sky. There was a buzz of excitement, catcalls. Some people threw things; it was like a fair. Vendors were offering hot sausages and cold drinks; the saloons were obviously doing good business. Men stood outside and toasted George as he passed.

The biggest crowd was outside the courthouse; a new building with stone outside and wood inside and plain furniture.

George was hurried through the crowd into the courtroom.

The fat deputy murmured, 'They'll give yuh more room when you shit your britches — as you will when yuh drop.'

George was put in the dock and left to wait as the deputies let in the jury and tried to control the over-eager crowd.

George looked searchingly at the jurymen; all were men who spent their time drinking in saloons. He tried not to show his discouragement. It was a test of his faith, he decided; so he put his trust in the Lord and murmured a prayer under his breath. Where was Toby? He looked around the room but his brother hadn't appeared.

Polly was right at the back, in a corner with the sheriff's wife. She smiled encouragingly at him.

Judge Benson strode in, his black robe swinging like bat's wings, and took his seat in front of the flag. He slammed his gavel down.

'Silence in court!'

Talk faded away as he glared around the room.

'I will have order in my court. Deputies will remove any son of a bitch causing a commotion of any kind.' He paused. 'It won't do any good that I can see, but we should observe the form of the law. Is anyone present prepared to stand up for the prisoner?'

The silence lasted long enough to suggest that no-one would speak for George. Then an unfamiliar voice said,

'I will, your honour.'

Necks craned to look at the stranger. Benson said, 'Your name?'

'Robert Frederick.'

'Are you a lawyer, Mr Frederick?'

'No, sir.'

'Do you have experience of court procedure?'

'I have, your Honour.'

'Very well. This court has no objection to Mr Frederick representing the accused, so let's get on with it. Call the first witness.'

Frederick said, 'Sir, I need time to consult my client about his defence.'

Benson frowned. 'I will grant you five minutes. Court will remain in session.' He sat fuming as Frederick walked up to the dock.

'You'd best tell me your side of things quickly, Mr Small.'

George didn't know who this stranger was or why he was taking his side, but he went through that evening one more time: hearing the shots and finding the body, a glimpse of a man vanishing into an alley, picking up the gun and the sheriff's arrest.

Frederick turned to the judge.

'The accused pleads 'not guilty' your Honour.'

Benson scowled. 'It doesn't matter what he pleads. Let's have the facts, Sheriff Nash.'

'Deputy Marshal Beaumont was shot

206

twice in the back. I heard the shots and ran towards the sound. I found the accused standing over the body with the gun in his hand.'

Benson was pleased.

'Thank you, Sheriff. That's clear enough for anyone. The prisoner's obviously as guilty as hell.'

'Objection, your Honour. My client says he saw another man disappearing into an alley. This was likely the real murderer.'

'Horse-shit! A made up story if I ever heard one.' Benson turned on the sheriff. 'Did you see anyone else at that time?'

'No sir. Main Street was deserted at that time.'

Frederick tried again. 'I suggest that the sheriff arrived afterwards — '

Benson glowered at him.

'I'm running this court, and I'm running it my way. I'll stand no nonsense from you, Mr Frederick, or anyone else. So don't try to prolong this session.'

Frederick persisted. 'Can the sheriff produce the murder weapon?'

'Well, Mr Nash, can you?'

'Yes sir, I have it here.'

The sheriff held out a revolver and Benson glanced casually at it. Frederick took it in his hand and inspected it closely.

'A Colt .45, well worn, obviously some years old. Mr Small, does this gun belong to you?'

'Of course not,' George said. 'I've never owned a gun in my life.'

'Is that it?' Benson's temper was as short as a burning fuse. 'You are wasting the court's time, Mr Frederick, and a lot of good people are waiting for the main event.'

Frederick looked at George and shrugged hopelessly.

Judge Benson turned to the jury benches and scanned each face there. His gimlet eyes bored into each one as if daring them to contradict him.

'Gentlemen of the jury, you have heard the evidence provided by Sheriff

Nash — ignore the rambling of this stranger. Before you stands a convicted killer and there is only one verdict you can bring in — '

'Guilty,' chanted the jurymen, almost as a chorus.

Benson's face relaxed in a smile.

'You, Mr Small, have been found guilty of murder and it is my duty to order you to be hanged by the neck until you are dead, dead, dead!'

Amongst the cheers and stamping of feet, Polly began to cry.

18

The Hanging

Millie and Monty went through the outskirts of Snake City at a brisk trot, as if they sensed this was an occasion. But when they reached Main Street they were forced to slow down. The broad, dusty highway was clogged with excited people.

Flags adorned false fronts and bunting was strung overhead from side to side. Folk chatted with their neighbours, and there were wagons with whole families from surrounding farms. Vendors were selling hot pies and pork chops.

Toby began to wonder if he'd lost track of the calendar and this was the fourth of July.

He tried to get his wagon through the crush, but people were reluctant to move; it seemed they thought he was just trying to get a better position.

Forced almost to a standstill, he asked, 'What's going on?'

A bystander shouted cheerfully, 'They're hanging that murderer who backshot the marshal.'

Toby swore, and did something he rarely did. He took up his whip and struck the mules. Their heads turned towards each other as if in surprise. Then they got the message: a special effort was needed. They put their heads down and pulled.

Folk who didn't get out of the way got trodden on, to the immense satisfaction of Millie and Monty. Wagon wheels threatened to crush bones of those who didn't move fast enough.

Ambrose saw what was needed and forced his horse up front to join Ella; together they cleared a path, pushing the crowd aside.

Ella fired her rifle over their heads, shouting, 'Make way, make way!'

Reluctantly, people moved and, gradually, Toby brought the wagon up to the foot of the gallows. He saw his brother standing on the platform, a noose around his neck.

'Stop!' Toby shouted. 'Stop the hanging! You've got the wrong man and I can prove it.'

Sheriff Nash stepped forward, frowning.

'Not you again. The judge has already found this man guilty and condemned — '

Ella raised her rifle and carefully shot through the rope above George's head. The loose end fell about his shoulders and the volunteer hangman backed away.

'Mr Wallace,' Toby called. 'Quickly, please — tell the sheriff what you know.'

Ella and Ambrose scrambled up on the wagon and helped the injured Easterner forward, where he could speak directly to the sheriff.

'Sheriff, the man who shot your marshal — and he boasted to me about it — was the same one who ruined my feet with a hot iron. He was foreman at the . . . '

People at the back of the crowd began to shout as they became impatient. 'What's going on? Why don't they hang the bastard? Are those strangers helping the prisoner escape?'

It seemed a riot might develop.

Wallace pulled the blanket from his feet. 'Can you read the brand?'

Nash bent over to read the cattle brand seared into the soles of both feet.

'That's plain enough . . . Crooked L. Are you telling me Carver did this?'

'He did,' Wallace said grimly, 'and now he's dead.'

He spoke seriously to the sheriff. By the time he'd finished, Nash said respectfully:

'That puts things in a different light.'

Toby jumped up on the platform as Nash unlocked the handcuffs.

'About time too,' George grumbled. 'What took you so long?'

'This and that.' Toby was itching to get down there among the crowd, selling his patent elixir. 'You know how it is.'

'I know how it is with you,' George said quietly. 'Thanks.'

Judge Benson was beginning to worry.

'If you turn the condemned man loose, Mr Nash, we're liable to have trouble.'

'I can't hang an innocent man, Judge.'

Robert Frederick stepped up on to the gallows platform, and now he was wearing a gunbelt. 'If yuh need help, Sheriff, I'll lend a hand.' He studied Wallace. 'This foreman — are yuh sure he's dead?'

'I'm sure. Miss Ella put a bullet in him; but there's still the man who gives the orders and hides behind a mask.'

'Reckon I know who holds a mortgage on the Crooked L,' Nash drawled, looking out over a sea of faces, searching for one in particular.

Ray had been watching the crowd, fascinated. Some were cheering because an innocent man had been freed; others were angry at being cheated of the thrill they'd expected. As he watched, a well-dressed man at the back of the crowd slipped away; and Ray eeled between close-packed people after him.

★ ★ ★

Whit Chancellor could scarcely believe his eyes when he saw Wallace showing his burned feet to Sheriff Nash. The shock of that moment riveted him to the ground. His head whirled. What had gone wrong? How had he escaped? Where were those fools, Harknett and Carver?

He felt betrayed. Wallace was a serious threat; he would be exposed and charged with kidnapping. And, of course, he'd known George Small was innocent and, if it hadn't been for this last-minute reprieve, would have allowed him to hang. Nash wouldn't like that.

He began, slowly, to edge his way out

of the crowd. People around him were chanting, 'We want a hanging,' and he started sweating, remembering another mob when the situation got out of his control.

It was then that he'd left the South in a hurry, after selling a ranch that didn't belong to him. The rancher and the man who'd paid him the money had got together and chased him long past the county line.

He'd have to run for it again, grab the loot from the bank, and get away to start somewhere else under another name. It was the pattern of his life.

His heart was hammering and his throat was dry as he hurried to the livery stable, saddled a horse and hitched him outside the bank.

He unlocked the door and went straight to his office, his pulse racing. He took out a gun from a drawer in his desk; no one was going to stop him now, no one. He picked up a couple of saddle-bags and carried them to the safe and unlocked it. He stuffed bank-notes and gold coins into the bags, puffing because he was out of breath.

As he turned to leave he saw the boy, and said, 'You! Get out of my way, boy!'

Ray recognized the voice.

'You're the man in the mask,' he blurted out.

It was another shock. Chancellor dropped one bag, brought up his gun and pointed it at Ray. His teeth bared in a wolfish grin.

'Too bad — '

Ray heard a gunshot, and flinched. Then he found he was still alive. It was the bank-robber who howled. His gun was on the floor with the saddle-bags and he was holding a hand that dripped blood. A bullet had ripped away flesh and shattered the bone in his trigger finger.

'Reckon it's the end of the trail for you, Chancellor, or whatever your name is,' Robert Frederick said from behind Ray. 'Figure you can carry those bags to the sheriff, son?'

'You bet,' Ray said. 'This is the man

who ordered me and Ella killed in an accident. He's the boss behind the Crooked L.'

'Guess we'll get it sorted out in time,' Frederick drawled, and prodded Chancellor with his revolver.

'Start walking back to where the sheriff is. There's nothing I'd like better than to gun yuh down, so it's fine with me if yuh make a break for your horse. Bo was a friend of mine.'

Chancellor was in too much pain to argue, though he cast a longing glance at his horse by the hitching rail. He felt the pressure of Frederick's big Colt in the small of his back.

'Try it . . . *please!*'

He walked slowly, thinking. *I'm too old for this*, towards the gallows. Ray followed close behind carrying the saddle-bags. On the gallows platform, the sheriff and Judge Benson were besieged by an angry crowd demanding a hanging.

Frederick used Chancellor as a ram to force a path through towards the sheriff.

'Mr Nash,' he called. 'This is the man you want. He's the one who gave the order to kill Beaumont — I caught him making a break for it with his loot.'

He took the bags from Ray and handed them up. He fished a US marshal's badge from his pocket.

'Bo was investigating Chancellor's bank, where ransom money was paid in. I'm continuing that investigation, and hunting Bo's killer.'

Chancellor looked sick and mumbled: 'You can't pin anything on me. You've got no proof.'

Immediately, Wallace shouted, 'That voice, I'd know that voice anywhere. He's the one who was hiding behind a mask . . . '

Ella added, 'I agree with Mr Wallace — there's no mistaking that voice. He's the one who ordered us killed!'

Chancellor struggled uselessly as Nash handcuffed him; the sheriff spoke to Benson.

'Can we afford to disappoint these good people, Judge? If we insist on a

regular trial, that means a delay —
there's likely to be a lynching party, and
I don't want that.'

Benson showed his teeth in a cruel
smile.

'My pleasure, Sheriff.'

He turned to the crowd but had a job
to make himself heard till Frederick
fired a shot over their heads.

'I've heard the witnesses,' Benson
said quickly, 'and I find the accused
guilty of — '

His voice was drowned in a savage roar:
'Hang him high!'

Nash nodded to the hangman to
proceed.

The hangman adjusted the knot in
the noose, and murmured, 'You got a
last prayer, now's the time.'

Toby put his hand on Ray's shoulder.

'You don't have to watch this. Take
Millie and Monty to the livery stable
and give them a good feed — I reckon
they deserve it.'

Ray had been about to protest when
Frederick said:

'I'll give you a hand, son.'

He jumped down and helped get the mules through the crowd as, behind them, a great roar went up. Ray opened a sack of oats and fondled their ears as Millie and Monty settled down happily to the meal of a lifetime.

Ray was puzzled. 'You missed the hanging, Marshal, yet Bo was your friend.'

'I'm sure he won't kill again — and nothing can bring Bo back.'

'But the judge, deciding just like that?'

'Waal, I guess it wasn't strictly legal today — but that crowd was over-excited and Benson is an old-timer. He worked the Territories. You know about them?'

'Sure. They were where the outlaws hid.'

Frederick nodded. 'Right. They used those places to hide from the law — wild men, killers, bank-robbers every one. Benson and a few marshals cleaned them out, and he got so he thought he was the law — and maybe that wasn't a bad thing then. But times change, and he'll be retiring soon.'

He watched Ray with the mules. 'You're good with animals, son, and I like that. Could be a job waiting for yuh with my office when you've grown a bit. Think you'd like that?'

'You bet!'

Frederick smiled. 'I'll fix it, partner.'

The crowd was thinning around the gallows as folk, still talking animatedly, drifted towards Snake City's saloons and dining-rooms. Behind them, the body of Whit Chancellor dangled at the end of a rope.

Ella looked around and saw some of the homesteaders — those who'd mortgaged their farms to the bank, she guessed — viewing the body with grim satisfaction.

Ambrose, unshaved and dusty, smiled at her. 'You've got a real story for your paper, Ella. I don't suppose . . . ?'

She felt a moment's regret.

'Sorry, no.'

There was an interruption when Polly started her pains and Anna whisked her away.

George and Owen Nash glanced at each other, and George said, 'I don't suppose it can be worse than what's already happened.'

'What we need is a drink,' Nash said.

'But I don't . . . ' George reconsidered. 'Well, it is a special occasion.' They went off together.

Ambrose studied Ella, and sighed; he turned to Wallace and murmured, 'So I'll be travelling back East with you.'

From the platform, Ella looked into the crowd, searching for Toby. She frowned when she saw him offering bottles of his elixir for sale, giving his spiel and taking money.

She jumped down and made for him.

'Just what d'you think you're doing?'

'Waal, I — '

There was an edge to her voice now. 'Because if you figure on going back to your old life, forget it. I want to settle down.'

Toby Small was, for one moment, tongue-tied, and she continued, 'So if we're going to settle down together, you'll need to reform.'

'Waal, shucks, of course I will, Ella.' His tongue recovered its usual glibness. 'Always reckoned to reform when I finally settled. Sure, I'll promise to reform any way you want, Ella . . . '

He gathered her in his arms and kissed her in the shadow of the gallows.

' . . . Trust me!'

We do hope that you have enjoyed reading this large print book.

Did you know that all of our titles are available for purchase?

We publish a wide range of high quality large print books including:
Romances, Mysteries, Classics
General Fiction
Non Fiction and Westerns

Special interest titles available in large print are:
The Little Oxford Dictionary
Music Book, Song Book
Hymn Book, Service Book

Also available from us courtesy of Oxford University Press:
Young Readers' Dictionary
(large print edition)
Young Readers' Thesaurus
(large print edition)

For further information or a free brochure, please contact us at:
Ulverscroft Large Print Books Ltd.,
The Green, Bradgate Road, Anstey,
Leicester, LE7 7FU, England.
Tel: (00 44) 0116 236 4325
Fax: (00 44) 0116 234 0205

THE SAVAGE RIVER

Sydney J. Bounds

The Pinkerton supervisor told Savage that the job was not dangerous. He must find Miss Beatrice Bottomley, a schoolteacher lost in the wild west. But along the way Savage is jailed, hunted by killers and shot twice. All because Bea was abducted by Foxy Parker's gang of gold robbers. But why is she so important to them? Although Savage faces constant danger, he remains undaunted. His guile, courage and expertise have always helped him win through — but will he succeed now?